HOUSE OF THE BLUE LILACS

HOUSE OF THE BLUE LILACS

Kelly Kathryn Griffin

For kelly,

Enjoy!

Kelly Kathryn Griffin

Writers Club Press
New York Lincoln Shanghai

House of the Blue Lilacs

Writers Club Press
an imprint of iUniverse, Inc.

For information address:
iUniverse, Inc.
2021 Pine Lake Road, Suite 100
Lincoln, NE 68512
www.iuniverse.com

ISBN: 0-595-25433-0

Printed in the United States of America

This book is dedicated to Eileen Lawson and Zane Spencer, whose editing and comments made this book possible!

CHAPTER 1

It is a beautiful day in late May. I place my crisp dress shirts in my hanging garment bag and snap shut my suitcase. My black mourning suit was brought out of its hiding place after I received the not unexpected phone call. I thumb through my tie collection and select a few subdued ones that will fit the occasion of a wake and funeral and add them to the garment bag.

It is Thursday morning and I have already called into the office and explained that I will need a few days off to pay my last respects to a dear friend. My wife, Lisa, has already left for work and Sarah and Andy, our two elementary aged children, have long since boarded the bus to school.

I open the small wooden, velvet-lined box on my dresser to select a tie clip to finish my somber attire. My searching eyes come to a stop over a pair of cuff links with a matching tie clip. I gently lift the cuff links out and look at them. They are silver and inlaid with a glossy mother-of-pearl, true works of art. They belong to a bygone era and I don't even remember ever owning a shirt that used cuff links. I place them back into the box and pick up the matching clip and attach it to the pocket of my knit shirt. Safest place for it, I think to myself. I close the lid to the box. I know I will pass the jewelry on to my son, not because they serve a practical purpose, they don't, but because of the precious memories that are carried with them.

I zip up the garment bag and swing it over my arm and pick up the suitcase in my other hand and make my way down the staircase. I pause by the front door and set the security alarm before I leave, locking the door behind me. My car sits in the driveway, my wife's car seemingly more deserving of any available space in the garage. I stow my belongings in the trunk and mentally plan how I wish to make this trip back to my boyhood home. In a way I am glad to be by myself in this journey. My wife will join me late tomorrow evening, bringing the children with her.

Backing out of the driveway I begin the long journey home. Even though rush hour is over, traffic in suburban Detroit never seems to slack off. I finally find my way to I-75 and put my driving skills into automatic as my mind continually drifts away from the present to the past and back again. The strip malls and endless subdivisions from Pontiac to Saginaw blend into one. It is only after turning into U.S. Route 10 that I truly see the farmland and gently rolling land-scape. I stop for a much-needed lunch and gas fill-up in the town of Clare. As I sit in the restaurant, I watch Amish buggies drive by. The quaintness of the scene is one more reminder of the much slower pace of life I once knew.

Lunch over, I head out again to Route 10 and hit State Route 115 and follow it past Cadillac to State Route 37. It is late afternoon and the sun has taken a decided dip in the spring sky as I near Traverse City.

My route takes me past Madison Street, the road that would lead me to my boyhood home on 45th Street. Deciding to come back the next day, I continue on my way to Raven Hill. Rush hour, such as it is in Traverse City this time of year, is in full swing and I am forced to slow down. I pass the downtown area and continue on State Route 37 to the Old Mission Peninsula jutting into the Grand Traverse Bay. About two miles past the city I find the private drive to Raven Hill and follow the dirt road to its end. Even though I have seen the house hundreds of times I am always impressed when I look upon

the Victorian style mansion. The steep pitch of the roof, the gingerbread decorated gables, the wraparound porch. It has never stopped
taking my breath away since I first saw it as a child riding in a speed-
boat below the bluffs.

Several cars and trucks are parked on the sides of the driveway
and I pull into a spot behind one of them and park. The air is decidedly much more brisk on the peninsula and I am glad I included my
lightweight jacket in the items to bring and I put it on when I step
out of the car. I dig out my luggage and make my way to the house. I
can see and hear people congregating in various parts of the large
home and I feel like an intruder and stand uncertainly at the door.
Before I can gather enough courage to turn the knob the door is
flung open by a young man who welcomes me with "Mr. Thorpe!
Come in, my mom has been waiting for you." It takes me a minute to
recognize the young man as Benjamin Van Raalte; it has been years
since I had last seen him. He must be around 20 years old. He insists
on taking my bags and disappears up the stairs with them.

I find myself alone once again, but not for long, as I am soon
greeted with a warm hug and a peck on the cheek. She holds me at
arms length and looks me over. I know immediately who it is; Fair
Emily. She is nearly as tall as I am as I look into the familiar blue eyes
that are framed by a short blonde do. The years have done little to
extinguish the beautiful young woman I remember. She takes me by
the hand and introduces me to dozens of people milling through the
rooms. I am reintroduced to her husband, Jack Van Raalte, Esquire,
and to her three younger children. Second in age to Benjamin is seventeen year old Sydney, fifteen year old Jason, and Brittney, eleven.

"The gathering tonight will be over in an hour. The memorial service is at 3pm tomorrow and we will hold that in the living room if
the weather is bad. Outside on the lawn if the weather cooperates.
That will be followed by a catered light supper. I think the caterer
said she would be here by two tomorrow to set up. The funeral is at
10am Saturday at the Old Stone Church. The graveside service will

immediately follow and the final gathering will be at Oak Lawn after that. It will be a busy few days," she finished with a sigh.

"I know she would have loved this gathering of her friends…and family."

Emily smiles at me and reaches over and squeezes my hand. We talk about the years that have gone by since we last saw each other, which must have been eight, when Emily's grandmother, Lydia Vanneste died.

By nightfall the people have all left except for Fair Emily, her family, her father and Mr. Griekos, the ancient handyman/gardner who looked after the grounds of Raven Hill for over five decades. It is not until everything has been checked twice does Emily announce that she is ready to call it a day and head for Oak Lawn, her grandmother's former estate located in Traverse City.

"Did I tell you that I had Sydney put fresh sheets on your bed and tidy up the room and bath for you?"

"Yes," I assure her. Sydney rolls her eyes behind her mother's back, just as she did the last time her mother asked me the same question.

The whole group walks Mr. Griekos to the small apartment behind the garage. We make sure he is settled in safely for the night. His wife, the lovely Mrs. Rose, has long since passed away.

"I don't know what will happen to him," worried Emily.

"Now Hon, you know he will always have a home here. He won't have to leave and someone will always be here to check in on him," comforts her husband.

"Yes, but he will miss Cleary."

"We will all miss Cleary," echoes Jack.

Taking advantage of the topic of conversation, I speak up. "What will happen to Raven Hill?"

"Oh there is going to be a big announcement at Oak Lawn on Saturday. Can you wait that long?" she teased.

"Well, I don't know…" I tease back.

The seven of them pile into a large sports utility vehicle and I wave goodbye. The sun has long since gone down when I make my way back up the drive to the house. I circle the porch until I can locate the stairs in the darkness. I stand on the porch and overlook the Grand Traverse Bay. While I can't see the water I can hear the regular lapping of the water on the rocks below the high bluff. In the distance, across the water I can make out the lights of the town of Acme. The stars come out one by one and I stand there, lost in my own thoughts. The familiar lingering scent wafts from the lilac bushes clustered about the lawn sloping down to the drop off over the lake. After an hour or so I finally rise up and make my way into the house. I remember I haven't eaten since lunch and I find a platter of lunchmeat left behind by the earlier gathering. I help myself to some food and find a glass in the cupboard for some water. I polish off my makeshift meal at the kitchen table. I examine the leaf pattern imbedded in the linoleum tabletop. It is the same table that I sat down to as a child. I look around the kitchen and I'm not surprised that it looks very much like it did that winter day when my father brought me to Cleary's door during that difficult time.

The cellular phone emits a dial tone when I turn it on and I tap in my home phone number and wait for someone to answer. My eight year old son, Andy, answers on the fourth ring and after he hands the phone over to Lisa, I tell her I made it safely to Traverse City and the memorial service is at 3pm Friday. My responsibilities over for the night, I take a quick tour of the main floor to make sure all the lights are turned off and the doors shut before I head up the stairs to the second floor. I surprise myself by remembering where the light switches are located. The top floor is L-shaped with thick, wooden doors leading to several rooms. The first room to my right at the top of the stairs is the room I stayed in all those years ago and I will stay in now. Directly across the hall is a large bathroom with the old metal tub I remembered so fondly. I open the closet in my bedroom and find my hanging clothes have been placed there. My suitcase is set next to the bed. The room shows signs of having been recently dusted and vacuumed. Bless that Sydney, I think to myself.

Feeling restless, I decide to look over the rest of the second floor. I step outside my door and continue down the hallway. The first door to my left is a large linen closet that I find stuffed with towels and sheets of every description. Across the hall from the linen closet is a small bedroom, much like the one I am occupying. Before the hall takes a turn to the left, there is another door that leads to the stairs up to the attic. I take the turn in the hall and see the door to Cleary's bedroom straight ahead. I head for it, passing two more bedrooms on the way. I flip on the light and find the room much as I remembered. The bed had been stripped and the slight smell of antiseptic hung in the air. I wondered if Sydney had also cleaned this room, the room where Cleary had died. The heavy, ornate furniture is among the finest I have ever seen. I pull open one of the upper drawers of the dresser, and embossed in the cherry wood are the familiar words "Calloway Furniture Company, Grand Rapids, Michigan". Her belongings are still in the drawers and closet. While the furniture has been polished, personal items such as her combs and brushes are still placed out in the open, as if their owner is expected home at any time. Large braided rugs are placed here and there on the solid, wooden floors. Her jewelry case still sits on the top of her dresser. I pull open the bottom drawer and gently look through the items jumbled inside. I do not find a key.

I begin to feel like an intruder and leave the room, turning off the light and shutting the door on the way out. Before I reach my room, I pass the one door I haven't opened yet. I gently turn the knob and reach for the string that will turn on the light. The narrow, steep stairwell lies before me. I slowly climb the stairs and listen to the creak and groans that I so well remember from my boyhood when I sneaked up these same steps. I pull the string to turn on the light when I arrive at the top of the steps and the dim bulb barely cuts into the gloom. I can make out a stack of old suitcases and trunks that are covered with stickers from foreign lands. Other boxes are stacked neatly around the room. On one of these stacks sits a small wooden box that I remember so well. I cross over to it and lift the lid. It is unlocked. I peer in and find it empty and I shut the lid. I think to myself that I shouldn't be surprised, the mystery that had cast a shadow over the whole community had long since been solved.

The events of the day are catching up to me as I make my way back down the stairs and back to my room. After unpacking my suitcase and slipping into bed, I turn off the lamp and quickly fall asleep in the familiar surroundings.

CHAPTER 2

Friday dawns sunny and clear and I feel like driving around before the memorial service and my father and sister arrive. After parallel parking the car, I eat breakfast at a small café downtown and watch the people walk by. The season is still early for tourists, but the "snowbirds", the retired people who live here just during the pleasant months, were probably already back to stay until fall.

Traveling a roundabout route to stay off the busier main roads, I find my boyhood home. I try to drive by every time I come to Traverse City, which by my recollection was nearly five years ago. The area around the neighborhood is all built up now. When I was a boy, the subdivision seemed to be on the outskirts of town and since most of the lots were not built on, it was almost like living in the country. But in the last twenty years all of the lots have been built on and the city has even spread to this corner of the world.

The house itself is nondescript. Built in the late fifties, it is a simple rectangle with a finished basement. Consisting of approximately 1700 square feet of living space on the main floor, it is divided into three bedrooms, two baths, living room and an eat-in kitchen. It even has a two-car garage, although we always had so much stuff stored in there that it was an effort to get in even one car. I smile to myself as I think that some things never change.

The current owners have painted it a pale yellow with dark green shutters, a move that would have horrified my mother if she were still living. While we lived there it had been a more modest white with dark blue shutters. The back yard was a good size and is now fenced in. The trees my parents had planted were now mature and towered over the house. I look at a clump of lilacs near the curb and I notice that they are nearly in full bloom. The blossoms are a pale violet color. My mother had taken the trouble to obtain a clump of lilacs from Cleary's yard, hoping that they too would be the famous blue color. But no, these too were simply the common violet color. No one had been able to duplicate the lilacs from Raven Hill and no one could ever figure out why.

I put the car into gear and head back to Raven Hill. I nearly turn into the drive before another idea comes to me and I continue north on State Route 37. I pass the tiny towns of Mapleton and Old Mission and continue on until the road ends. I park my car in the empty parking lot and get out. The wind is quite brisk and I zip up my jacket. I walk to the path leading to the Old Mission Lighthouse. No one is around, so I assume the caretaker is out on other business. A boardwalk skirts the lighthouse and leads to a sandy beach. The water this time of year is icy cold and once you step off the sandy beach, is extremely rocky. Much better suited to be enjoyed from the beach than from the water. I take a seat on a bench and watch the seagulls swoop across the water. The bright sun makes me sleepy and I close my eyes and enjoy the sounds of the birds and the water hitting the shore. The air has the mixed scent of water and seaweed rotting on the sand. You certainly couldn't enjoy this atmosphere in Detroit, even along the river.

A glance at my watch reveals that it is nearly one o'clock and my father and sister are to meet me at Raven Hill at one-thirty. I stand up and brush off the sand from my clothes and hurry to my car. Even though I arrive before one-thirty I find my father's car parked in the driveway at Raven Hill. I hurry into the house to find them. My sister

Debbie answers my greeting and I find her in a downstairs bathroom putting on her make-up.

"Where is Dad?"

"Upstairs getting changed. He is very upset, but handling it OK, I guess," she answers my unasked question. I climb the stairs so that I too can get dressed. My dad's belongings are in one of the bedrooms, but he is nowhere to be found. I quickly walk the hall and find him in Cleary's room. He is standing in front of her chest of drawers and looking at a picture sitting there. He glances in my direction and gives me a sad smile.

"Do you remember this picture, Kevin?"

"How could I forget." I look at the group of happy youths in the picture. My dad is in the picture, so is Cleary. We stand there looking at it for a few minutes before I break the silence. "I think we need to get ready Dad." He nods in reply.

Later we find Debbie, hands on hips, waiting for us at the bottom of the stairs when Dad and I had finished dressing. "And you guys talk about US! People are already arriving, the caterer is here, and the people from the funeral home are setting up outside since it's so nice out."

Dad and Debbie decide to join the people in the backyard and see what they can do to help the caterers and the people from the church. I head out the front door and find Fair Emily taking charge of the situation. She had directed Benjamin and her husband to deal with the long line of cars streaming onto the property while she greeted everyone with a warm hug and a few kind words before ushering them to the backyard. She asks me to stay with her and help greet the mourners. I do this gladly as I recognize most of the guests as people I grew up with and I hadn't seen most of them in years, if not decades.

It is after 3 o'clock when little Brittney approaches us and tells us the service is about to begin. We find most of the people seated in the chairs facing the lake, while a few are standing off to the side. Placed at the rear of the chairs are tables overflowing with flowers; also on the tables are dozens of pictures. Snapshots of Cleary, Cleary with friends, Cleary with relatives. I absently flip through the pages of the guest book and find only the last page empty. As I look at the scene before me, I think that anyone would be led to believe that this woman had been beloved by everyone all her life; however, I know that this is not the case.

Reverend Jameson, a young minister in his first assignment, begins the service with prayers before moving on to the remembrances we share with each other. When it is my turn to speak I unconsciously fiddle with my silver and mother-of-pearl tie clip. I tell of her attending my college graduation in Ann Arbor. What it meant for her to come all that way. I tell of the story behind the gift she gave me, a pair of mother-of-pearl cuff links and matching tie clip. It is a story most of them already know.

After the service the catered food is displayed on the long tables set out on the wide porch. The afternoon passes quickly as I reacquaint myself with several friends and ex-neighbors. I discover that Ted now owns his own construction company, Barb has five children and is planning her own art show in Chicago. Alan, the class trouble maker, is now a policeman in Grand Rapids. Gradually the crowd thins and my father and Mr. Griekos drift off to the older man's apartment to relax after the busy day. Debbie decides to join some childhood friends for a movie and leaves for the city. Emily and her family are the last to leave, after making sure the house and grounds are back in order for the final services tomorrow.

I decide to relax on the porch swing and stare out over the calm, blue water of the bay. The peace doesn't last long. I hear a car pull up in the driveway and in a minute Andy and Sarah descend upon me. Lisa is close behind them and inquires about the memorial service. While the children run off to explore the grounds, I catch her up on the news.

While I am telling her that my dad was holding up quite well, she cocks her head to the side and says, "Are those the famous blue lilacs I smell?"

I assure her that it is indeed the lilacs producing the wonderful scent. We get up from the porch swing and walk across the lawn to an ancient clump of lilac bushes. She gently grasps several branches and pulls them closer to her face. "Why they really are blue! And the smell! I never quite believed you when you talked about them. But they really are the same color as my jeans."

We walk the expansive lawn and admire all of the lilacs; some are the more traditional white or purple. I tell her that several people have taken cuttings or sucker shoots and planted them elsewhere but they always bloomed into violet blossoms. Lisa asks how that could be possible.

I try to explain. "She said it was because of the soil, the water from the lake. She tried to tell me some things are just special in one place and if you take it out of that place then they are just ordinary." I don't quite know how to explain what Cleary had told me all those years ago. Luckily the sight of our children wading in the chilly water after we told them not to go there without our supervision distracts my wife.

After gathering up our children and finishing a tour of the property, we knock on Mr. Griekos' door and ask him and my dad to join us for dinner in the house.

We make an early evening of it and tuck the children into one of the small bedrooms. With dad in one room, Debbie in another, and Lisa and I in the fourth bedroom, it made for a full house. However, none of us had the heart to take Cleary's room. It would seem too disrespectful to move into her room so soon.

I lay wide-awake long after I hear the snoring and deep breathing of my family around me. I hear Debbie come in and make her way quietly to her room. If I shut my eyes, I am eleven again and remember what it was like to live here for that brief time. But when I allow myself back to the present day, I am forced to again realize that Cleary is gone. I drift off as the grandfather clock downstairs strikes midnight.

CHAPTER 3

❀

It is well past dawn before I stir in my twin bed. I open one eye to see if my wife is still asleep; however, I find the sheets pulled down and her missing. I trod quietly and check the other bedrooms. All of the beds are empty. For a moment I glorify in the sunlight streaming through the windows of the second floor and the peace and silence that surrounds me. But the reason I am back at Raven Hill dampens my joy and I head back to my bedroom and quickly dress in my jeans and a sweatshirt.

On the porch I scan the lawn and don't see a soul. On a hunch I walk to the edge of the lawn and look down. My family is climbing on the rocks on the lakeshore. I call to them as I make my way to the wooden staircase that winds down to the rocky beach.

"It's too bad it's not a sandy beach," remarks Lisa when I catch up to her.

It would be nice I agree but then add, "Cleary never did like change. The house is exactly the same as when I stayed here. I guess it helped her to remember…happier days."

My children try to wade in the cold water. "Ouch! I *hate* these rocks!" complains Sarah.

"Cleary always waded in an old pair of tennis shoes. Maybe the new owners will put in a sandy beach."

"Is Raven Hill for sale?" inquires Debbie.

"I don't know. I wish I could afford it."

She laughs. "Me too! I couldn't afford to mow the yard."

After walking for awhile I glance at my watch and notice that it is time to grab a fast breakfast and get dressed for the funeral. This news draws howls of protest from the children, which are quieted somewhat by the reminder that they would be coming back that evening and the next day.

We eat a simple breakfast of fruit and granola bars that Lisa had brought with her before we head off to our rooms to change into more suitable attire.

Lisa and I are dressed in the more traditional black, but for Sarah we allow her to wear the smocked flowered dress she had worn for Easter the month before. Andy wears his navy, and indeed his only, suit. I stand behind him, trying to knot his tie correctly. "Why don't you wear a clip-on?" I ask him. He gives me the darkest of looks and declares "Clip-ons are for *babies!*" With that he escapes my grasp and goes to his mother who is curling her hair in the bathroom. A minute later he is back with a perfectly knotted tie and a smile on his face. For a minute I am taken back in time when I look at the triumphant look on his face. I shake my head to come back to the present time and glance at my watch. It is nearly 10:30 and time to go.

We find Mr. Griekos waiting for us on the porch and we all pile into two cars and drive to the Old Stone Church, Congregationalist. I pull up to the entrance and let my passengers out before I circle the block looking for a parking spot. I finally locate a space on one of the side streets and walk back to the church. I open the doors and make my way through the crowd in the foyer. To no one's surprise the pews are overflowing and it takes a minute to find my family near the front. The altar is covered with spring flowers and a sweet, cool breeze sweeps through the sanctuary from the open windows. Reverend Jameson starts a few minutes late, allowing latecomers to bring chairs from the basement and sit in the back of the sanctuary.

The service goes by quickly and at the end I stand up with several other men and make my way toward the casket in front of the altar. We line up on each side and as one lift up the casket and carry it down the aisle, down the front steps and to the waiting hearse. Others bring the baskets of flowers and place some in the hearse and others in another car belonging to the funeral home. The funeral home staff hands out little flags to place on our car for the procession to the cemetery.

The line of cars stretches for blocks and with the help from the local police department we manage to all stay together. Retracing the route I had taken just that morning, we pass the drive to Raven Hill and about a half-mile later enter the cemetery. We park in the order in which we entered, as there is no room to pull off to the side. The cemetery is rather small and old, some of the stones dating back to the 1800's and the stones read as a who's who of the by-gone days of Traverse City. The considerable number of mourners somehow manage to gather around the graveside.

I lean against a headstone and am startled when I read the name "Lydia Augusta Standish Vanneste". Who knew that one day Cleary would be laid to rest so close to the town matriarch, I muse to myself.

After a short service we head back to the car and the entire line of cars move as one out of the cemetery and head back to the final stop on our itinerary.

Not far from the Old Stone Church we park on a side street and walk toward a brick wall that encircles the nearly three acre estate that used to sit on the outskirts of town and now is surrounded by homes and small businesses. We come to an iron gate that is already open and pass through. My children, catching sight of the house for the first time, are entranced. Oak Lawn and Raven Hill, both built late in the Victorian period, are a study in contrasts. Raven Hill gives off a cozy feeling with its gingerbread trim and wraparound porch. Oak Lawn is a three-story majestic brick mansion, the somber architecture exuding wealth, yet practicality. Even the garden and lawns differ in personality. Raven Hill is dotted here and there with native plants and shrubs in an almost wild and unkempt setting. Oak Lawn is three acres of manicured lawn protected by a four-foot high brick wall. Formal gardens are precisely planted with exotic flowers and plants that are grown in the on-site greenhouse. We make our way to the house via a brick walkway lined with freshly planted flowers. We meet others making their way in from other entrances and enter by the back door. I am taken aback for a moment by the sign posted at the back door that reads, "Welcome to Oak Lawn." Of course I knew that the old mansion had become a Bed and Breakfast soon after the death of Mrs. Lydia Vanneste about eight years previously. Along with the death of Cleary, it was one more reminder of the disappearance of the boyhood I remembered. We enter a large empty foyer with a back staircase leading to the upper floors. We continue past the stairs and enter the main hallway that leads to the main rooms on the first floor. People are scattered about in small clumps. My family and I are hungry so we find the room with the food tables set up and get in line.

After we finish eating, I allow the children to head outside as long as they promise to stay within the brick walls. Lisa finds my father and Mr. Griekos and they try to find seats in the music room. I decide to wander around the rooms and see what changes had been made since I returned home for the funeral of Lydia Vanneste. I slip up the main staircase and reach the second floor. These were once the bedrooms of Lydia, her husband Donald and their two children, Frank and Robert. Now they are guestrooms and Emily, Frank's only child, is staying as a guest in her own grandmother's estate. I continue up to the third floor and look around. At one time it housed the live-in staff; now it contains four more guestrooms. I quietly walk down the narrow hallway to the back staircase. Surely it couldn't still be there. I switch on the lights that illuminate the steps and there on the walls are the photographs I remember seeing during the Christmas party so long ago. A few steps down is the photograph I am seeking. A set of stern-looking, middle aged parents with a young, blond girl between them. There she was, Lydia Vanneste, or should I say Lydia Standish, her name before she married. She is pictured as she was in 1910, five years old in a stiff white dress and a big bow tied in the back of her head. She stares directly out of the picture with a look of utter confidence and determination. I know that she would never lose that look throughout her life. And it would be a life that would hold its difficulties and heartbreak. That look would also lead others to think the worst of her; I know I did.

On the main floor I make my way to the east drawing room. During Christmas parties this room held the liquor and drinks for the children and I find that this hasn't changed; a small bar has been set up in one corner. The Victorian décor is much as it was that day of Benjamin's christening, with the English hunt prints and the overstuffed furniture. None of us attending that ceremony would ever dream that the secret of the town's most respected families would be revealed and culminate in the town coming together to bid farewell to Cleary.

I suddenly notice that the sounds of people eating and talking have come to an abrupt end in the other rooms and I go to investigate. I find Emily standing in front of the fireplace with everyone standing around her. I stand at the back of the circle and strain to hear her.

"…thank you again for coming here today for our last farewell to Cleary. I know there has been a lot of speculation of what was to become of Raven Hill after she was gone. Cleary thought about this a lot in her last months and I am happy to be able to say that her estate and the local hospice association have been able to come to an agreement. The house and grounds will be used for hospice patients who are unable to receive the needed care at home and don't wish to be in a hospital. Cleary hoped Raven Hill would be as much of a comfort to others as it was to her. Of course work will need to be done on the house and probably another building resurrected on the property too. Those details are still to be worked out."

The people standing about break into applause. Emily smiles warmly and continues, "I am happy to announce that Mrs. Norton will be heading up the committee to oversee the project." She hastily adds, "Of course I will be actively involved and will come in often from Chicago." As I drift away from the crowd, Emily goes on to introduce Mrs. Norton, a local society matron.

So Raven Hill would become a hospice. I am relieved that it isn't to become another high-priced resort like other large estates had become in increasingly popular Traverse City.

It is nearly dusk when we reach Raven Hill. Lisa and I each take a sleeping child, exhausted from running and playing on the grounds of Oak Lawn. My father and Debbie take Mr. Griekos to his apartment and make sure he is settled in for the night. After the children are changed into pajamas and tucked into their beds, I change into my jeans and a warm sweater. I tell Lisa that I will be back in a little while and walk down the stairs to the kitchen. I open a bottom drawer and just as I expected find a large flashlight. I make my way out of the door and follow the lawn to the lake. Before the steep drop off to the water, I turn north and shine my light into the thick woods and underbrush. I find the path I am looking for. The moon is so bright I decide to save my batteries and switch off my flashlight and follow the twists and turns by moonlight. Before long I step into a large clearing dotted by the eerie sight of headstones. The cemetery. I make my way to the mound of freshly dug earth and shine my light on the headstone that had been put into place years before. The date of death had not yet been inscribed but her name was. In bold letters it declared who was buried here: **Clarissa Elizabeth Calloway.**

I sit on the cement bench that was placed there for visitors to the family plot. I set the flashlight down next to me and stare up at the stars. My reverie is short lived, however, when I hear the sounds of chatter and footsteps coming from the path I had just followed. It is Lisa and the children.

"I am so sorry," she begins. "They heard you leave the house and wanted to know where you were going."

It is OK I assure her and I invite her to sit beside me. Sarah and Andy, dressed in sweats over their pajamas, sit at our feet.

"What are you doing here? Do you miss your friend?" asks Sarah.

"Yes, I do miss her. I wish I had seen her recently. I guess I didn't realize how sick she was." Or maybe I didn't want to know, I think to myself.

"Did you grow up together?"

I smile at the thought. "No, not with me. She did grow up with Grandpa Thorpe, but she was a friend of mine too."

"What was she like?"

"Well, when I first met her I thought she was rather eccentric."

"Huh?"

"Ahhhh…I thought she was rather odd. But I got to know her and what had happened to her."

"What happened to her? Was she in an accident or something?" broke in Andy.

"No, not an accident. Here, I'll start at the beginning, OK?"

Drawing a deep breath I look into their expectant faces and begin the story of my friendship with Cleary.

CHAPTER 4

I can't say there was a time when I didn't know who Cleary was, at least in name only. But I have to admit that the children of the town would refer to her as "Old Miss Calloway." As most families in the Bay area, my family owned a motor boat in which we spent many a summer day exploring the Grand Traverse Bay and beyond. We would motor slowly beneath the bluffs and gaze up at the houses and cottages that lined the shore. Our favorite house was the one known by the name Raven Hill and occasionally we would see a figure walking on the lawn. My father would peep the horn to get the person's attention. Once the person turned our way, my father would signal with waving his arm to the left and then quickly to the right twice quickly and then twice slowly. The figure would answer with the same code and if the winds were calm verbal greetings would be exchanged as well. The water below the bluffs was too shallow and rocky for us to come in too closely. Usually all I would see of the mysterious "Old Miss Calloway" was long flowing skirts and long hair held back by a ribbon.

I didn't get a closer view of her until the summer I was nine. The whole family had gone to downtown Traverse City to go shopping for college supplies for Kathy. It was soon apparent that my father and I were merely in the women's way. I sat on a bench in the park overlooking the Bay and kept an eye on the packages my mother and sisters had purchased up to that point. My father, taking advantage of being downtown, wandered off to the sportsman shop.

After soaking up the last of the summer's sunshine and watching the gulls beg for breadcrumbs from a group of girl scouts, my attention is directed at a solitary soul seated on another bench. She is facing me, about a hundred feet away. Her attention seems captured by the book her face is buried in. Her right hand is unconsciously playing with the long braid of hair draped over her shoulder. Her purple skirt is unfashionably long, meeting the tops of the white sport socks she is wearing with her sensible tennis shoes.

In such a small town, I knew a good number of the natives, even by age nine. I figured she must be either one of the many tourists that flocked to the area in the summer or perhaps one of the many wealthy people that had summer cottages in the area. She looks up suddenly when someone calls a name I do not catch. I notice a middle-aged man and a young woman walk up and start talking to her. She immediately puts the book to the side and motions for the couple to join her on the bench, which they do. I recognize her visitors as Frank Vanneste and his daughter Emily. Mr. Vanneste is the only surviving child of Mrs. Lydia Vanneste, the town's matriarch. He is the head of the largest law firm in the surrounding ten counties. The young woman is his only child and is known throughout the region as "Fair Emily." No one knew when she gained the addition to her name but it seemed to fit her so well that "Fair" was automatically attached to "Emily." She was tall, willowy, and dark lashes framed large sapphire eyes. A head full of white, blonde hair capped off all of this. But it was more than her looks; she had a carriage of a duchess and the sweetness of a saint. She would often babysit for my sisters and I in our younger years. She was always fun, letting us stay up late and popping corn for us and plying us well with soda.

As I watch the threesome, I see Fair Emily extend her left hand and show something on it to the older woman. Even from that distance I can see the excitement on the mysterious woman's face as she turns Emily's hand and I catch a flash from something on her finger. Even at that age I figure out what is causing all the excitement, a ring, an engagement ring I am sure. The Vannestes obviously knew this person well, as they proceeded to huddle closely together on the bench, chatting happily.

My observations are interrupted by my father returning from his shopping trip to the sportsman store. He carries a new fishing pole and holds it out for me to admire as he says, "Look Kev, I picked it up for half price. It will be a great replacement for the pole Kathy dropped overboard last week."

I admire his good bargain and he sits beside me. It is then he notices the group across from us. "Ah, there is Frank, Emily and Cleary. I should go say hello."

"Old Miss Calloway?" I ask.

He gives me a long look and replies, "That's not nice Kev, you should call her Miss Calloway."

Trying to change the topic, I add, "Fair Emily was showing her a ring."

"Hmmmm, I had heard rumors that Emily had gotten engaged to an up-and-coming lawyer in Chicago. Let's go take a look at that ring." As we stand up to make our way over to them, Mom and the girls returning from their shopping interrupt us. I can tell things did not go well as Mom wears a harassed look on her face and the girls appear not to be speaking to each other.

"What happened?" my father innocently inquires.

Kathy speaks first. Fuming she spits out, "Why did you bring *her* along? You are supposed to be buying stuff for *me*! And every time I turn around *she* is trying on a new dress or shoes! And…"

"I just got a new blouse and jeans! You get everything new! All I ever get are hand-me- downs! I just try on a few nice outfits and you complain about that!"

I sit back on the bench, knowing that this is an argument that will go on for several minutes and with neither side winning or happy with the outcome. I am not disappointed. After Mom has calmed both parties, Kathy whines, "I want to go home. NOW!"

"Well, we are going to the exhibit at the old photographer's studio after we put these packages in the car." The girls both start to whine and my mother intercedes with "We are going to do something I want to do! Come on!" She grabs Kathy's hand and drags her behind her. Debbie stomps after them and Dad and I look at each other wondering if we dare follow.

My father looks over at the now empty bench and comments, "I guess I will have to drop in on the Vannestes later this week. Come on Kev, we had better follow them."

We make it to the car just as Mom is slamming down the trunk. "Tom," she says to my father, "let's keep the parking space and walk to the photographer's studio, it's only a few blocks." We all agree, mainly because none of us want to be in the same car together at this moment.

We are surprised to find a large crowd of people milling outside the old studio. My parents see several people they know and say hello. We kids find a table serving punch and cookies and get in line.

"How are you kids doing?" I hear a voice behind me say. I look behind me and find Fair Emily with one arm around each of my sisters. "Did you see what I picked up the other weekend?" she says casually as she waves her left hand around in an exaggerated manner. My sisters squeal excitedly as they see the considerable diamond perched on a gold band. Their argument is quickly forgotten as they both quiz Fair Emily about the ring, fiancé, and the upcoming wedding. After obtaining a plastic cupful of punch and a chocolate chip cookie, I find my parents who are finally ready to go inside the exhibit.

The old photographer's studio is housed in an old section of town. The two-story building predates the turn of the twentieth century and is built with red brick. It has housed the Sullivan Photographic Company for over eighty years, spanning four generations of picture taking Sullivans. The studio had closed with the death of Owen Sullivan about five years previously and a small gift shop had run out of the main floor. It was only after the gift shop closed and the restaurant next door had wanted to expand into the space did anyone venture to the second floor and look over what had been left behind from its days as a photography studio. The second floor had yielded a treasure trove of old cameras of every description and boxes of photographs that spanned the history of the art from the late 1800's to the 1960's. After the value was assessed, a search was conducted to find living relatives who would claim ownership of the items. Only a handful of uninterested distant cousins were found and they signed ownership over to the local historical society.

After years of elderly volunteers going through the photographs and identifying the places and people whenever possible, the exhibit was to show off some of them with the donations going to the preservation of this local treasure find. The main floor was bare except for pillars and a few walls that were to be kept standing. The restaurant would wait until after the exhibit to tear down the dividing wall. On the walls were framed photographs with a small card placed underneath describing and identifying the subject. I munch on my cookie as I begin with the earliest photographs that contain a lot of horses and lumberjacks hauling some of the biggest trees I have ever seen in life or in pictures.

"It's hard to believe there were trees like that around Michigan," my father whispers to me, as if reading my mind.

"How come I haven't seen a tree like that around here?"

"There are a few places in Michigan where you can see trees like that, but most were logged years and years ago."

We travel together around the room, telling each other what we like most about the photos. Before we reach the first corner of the room we come across a photograph that I especially like. "What do you like most about it?" asks my father.

I look intently at the picture. It is a simple picture really, just a black and white picture of a girl in her early adolescence, jumping rope on top of a stopped train car. Her arms are raised with the jump rope and from the angle of the lens block most of her face, save her nose and chin. Her long blonde hair is pulled back with a large bow. She wears an ankle length sailor dress and while she is wearing long black stockings, she is shoeless. I look at the descriptive card and it states simply "Ca. 1915, South Boardman, Michigan. The Wild Girl of the Trains."

"I like it because it looks like you could see her face if you could just move your position." And I cocked my head off to the side. "And it also shows motion, the others look so…stiff…and…" And I struggle for the correct word.

"Staged?"

"Yes! That's it."

"Well, back then the film had to be exposed to light longer to take a picture, that's why most pictures look so staged. The people had to sit very still so the picture wouldn't look blurry. It must have been a very sunny day and she must have slowed the rope in order for him to take this shot."

"Where is South Boardman?"

"It's about an hour south of here. They did a lot of lumbering there around the time this picture was taken, so maybe she was related to one of the lumbermen, although she looks very well dressed." He looks again at the picture and raises his eyebrow. "You know…," but he never finished his sentence as right then a commotion behind us attracts our attention.

We turn to see Mrs. Lydia Vanneste standing in the middle of the room. She is a tall, full figured woman topped off with a large, billowing head of silver gray hair. She is known for her impeccable taste in clothing and today is no exception as she stands there in her navy linen suit. Her demeanor and clothing seems to suggest that she expects respect from others. Her cane that she carries with her demands it. Right now she is holding up her cane and shaking it at Old Miss Calloway, or should I say Miss Calloway. Her face is red and in an angry voice she states simply, "Now don't you start thinking that I am inviting *you* to the wedding!" Miss Calloway's jaw drops, along with Fair Emily's and her father's as they are standing directly behind Miss Calloway.

Miss Calloway responds by simply standing up straight, clenching her fists, and walking out the door. The old woman harrumphs and turns around to look at some photographs. Fair Emily bursts into tears and leaves the building with her father close behind.

The room falls completely silent after the young lady leaves the room. But Mrs. Vanneste seems oblivious to the silence as she continues to examine each of the photographs. After a few awkward moments, the banter picks back up. My father and I proceed to the later pictures, while glancing the old woman's way every few minutes. When she reaches the photograph of the girl skipping rope, she stops, adjusts the glasses on her nose and peers in for a better look. Then just as quickly she goes on to the next photograph. She must not have liked it, I think to myself as I turn back to a picture showing the victory celebration that the city held at the end of World War II.

"What was that all about?" questions Debbie in the car on the way home.

"Yea," chimes in Kathy. "I heard that Lady Vanneste just *hates* Old Miss Calloway. WOW does she ever!"

"Lady Vanneste?" says my father. "And stop calling her 'old Miss Calloway.' Cleary is only a year older than me, you know. Where do you kids get all this anyway?"

The girls continue as if he hadn't said a word. "She got so mad when she heard Fair Emily and Ol…Miss Calloway talking about the wedding. I was right behind them. Why did she get so mad about the wedding, doesn't she like the man Emily is marrying?" asks Kathy.

"I think it might be…" my father starts. My mother gives him a side look and a small shake of her head. My sisters are too busy trying to unravel the mystery of the fighting women to see the exchange between the two. I have no idea what it could mean. I thought weddings were happy occasions; why would the two be so angry about the event? I stare out the window and wonder if we will get an invitation to the wedding. Usually only adults went to such things and the wedding of my Aunt Tina last year had been a rather boring event. But for some reason, I think I want to see what will happen, plus Fair Emily is my favorite girl, after my mom of course, but definitely ahead of my sisters.

CHAPTER 5

That fall Kathy left for college in Indiana. The seven-hour drive to Indianapolis ensured that we would only be seeing her during major holidays. Debbie, sixteen, began her junior year of high school and I started fourth grade at the local elementary school. I was relieved to find Ted, Tony, and Alan, my neighbors and best friends since babyhood, placed in the same class I was. There were girls in the class, too, of course, but we didn't have much to do with them unless put under duress by the teacher.

It was that fall that the four of us boys began camping, a hobby that we would enjoy through high school. It began when Alan found an old canvas tent in his family's garage and invited the rest of us to help set it up in his back yard. One thing led to another and soon we were setting it up in each other's backyards and spending weekend nights in it. School nights were strictly off-limits for camping out. Early November was unusually balmy for northern Michigan and we are delighted that our camping season was to be extended for at least one more weekend. We decide to camp out in Ted's backyard that Friday night for two reasons—one it is his turn and two, unbeknownst to the other parents, his mother and father will be out of town. We won't be totally on our own; Ted's older brothers will be keeping an eye on us.

That Friday afternoon after school, I pack my backpack with the essentials—underwear, a change of clothing, and my toothbrush. I bid adieu to my unsuspecting parents and walk the mile to Ted's house. We set up the tent and go into the house for a dinner of canned spaghetti-O's and Tab, a treat we never would have had under adult supervision. After stuffing ourselves and considerately leaving the dirty dishes in the sink for Mrs. Johnson, Ted's mother, we pick up a few board games and a battery- operated lantern and head out the door to the tent to begin the night's entertainment. Before reaching the tent we can hear voices from the nearby field. In the remaining sunlight we follow the voices and find Ted's brothers, seventeen year-old Brian and fifteen year old Brad with Dan, a friend from the neighborhood. They are sitting in a circle talking and smoking Marlboro's which they quickly snuff out and toss away when they see the younger boys approaching.

"Watcha doin?" asked Ted.

"Jus talkin," answered Brian "Get outta here Squirt."

"Watcha talkin about?"

The older boys shrug their shoulders and Dan answers, "We were just talking about the going ons at the old cemetery."

"What's going on there?" piped up Alan.

"Strange lights are moving around there at night."

"I don't believe it," interjects Brad.

"No, really. Sandy and Fred swear they saw lights moving around the cemetery when they went fishing this last summer. Beat a hasty retreat I hear," insists Dan.

"Well, I'd like to hear what Sandy and Fred were doing fishing together," laughed Brad, and added, "and what they were fishing for?"

Tony spoke up. "I've heard about that too. Trina said that her aunt saw something a year ago in the cemetery. She thought it was a ghost."

At that they all laugh. When they sober up, Dan suggests, "Let's go up there tonight and check it out."

"It's a long walk," protests Brad.

"Well your parents are gone and you *do* have the keys to the second car don't you?"

"The station wagon? You want to be seen in that thing?" Brian asks incredulously.

"It's dark, and it's only a few minutes drive," persists Dan.

Brian leans back on one arm and thinks for a minute. "I do have my driver's license and Mom and Dad were saying I needed more practice behind the wheel...OK, I'll do it."

"Can we come?" asks Ted.

"No way!" exclaims Brad.

"I'll tell Mom you were smoking! And besides, if we are left alone we might burn the house down or something bad might happen to us," he coerces.

The older boys look at each other and roll their eyes before Brian speaks up. "OK, you can come. BUT you have to behave yourselves and if I tell you to shut up, then you'd better shut up. OK?"

The younger four of us nod our heads. Imagine! We are going on an adventure with 'big' kids. Life can't get better than that.

We wait until long after dark has fallen. It is nearly ten o'clock before the older boys decide they might have better luck seeing something strange going on at the cemetery. The seven of us pile into the station wagon and Brian orders all of us to put on our seat belts before he carefully backs the large car out of the driveway. He sits hunched over the steering wheel and slowly maneuvers the cumbersome vehicle down the street.

"Little nervous driving?" snickers Dan.

"Hey, I can't have an accident while my parents are gone and I promised not to use the car unless it was an emergency, now can I?" he snips back.

The chatter turns to speculation of what could be causing the ghostly lights.

"Maybe it's swamp gas," suggests one.

"What's swamp gas?" asks another and got "I don't knows" in response.

We finally drive out of town and up the narrow peninsula on State Route 37. The road is unlit and we can barely see 10 feet ahead of us as clouds obscure any light from the moon and stars. A porch light here and there are the only signs of civilization that we can see on our way to the cemetery.

"That's the drive to Raven Hill," Dan informs Brian. "So the cemetery must be right up here. Turn off the lights so you don't frighten off any ghosts."

Brian, even driving slowly, manages to miss the narrow lane to the cemetery.

"Never mind," assured Dan. "Just park on the side of the road and we can walk back."

I begin to wonder what I have gotten myself into as I look out the car windows and see total blackness, but it's too late now.

Brian eases the car to the shoulder and comes to a gentle stop and puts the car into park. "Whew. Made it," he says more to himself than to anyone else.

"We still have to go back home," comments Ted.

"Just shut up," was his answer to his baby brother.

"Shhhhh…We have to be quiet," commands Dan.

Together the seven of us slowly make our way back to the lane that leads to the cemetery. Some of us carry flashlights but don't turn them on so as to not give ourselves away. The cemetery is still and a quick look around tells us no one is about, at least not yet. Where to hide and wait for a ghost? After a hushed consultation we decide to hide beneath the sign posted near the entrance of the cemetery. The sign itself is about four feet by six feet and mounted on short posts. Painted on it are posted the rules and regulations of the operation, such as no plastic flowers and that it is closed for business at dusk. Since it faces the headstones rather than the visitors entering from the road, one could wonder which clientele the sign is meant for. Under the sign are planted a few bushes, which are bare of their leaves during this time of year, but because it is so dark, still affords a safe place to hide. The seven of us lay or squat behind the bushes, either looking through them or around them to detect any movement from the cemetery.

Time passes slowly and my eyes are beginning to droop. Suddenly Tony slaps my back and whispers, "Look there!"

From the woods opposite us we can see a light swinging through the trees. Collectively we take a sharp intake of breath and hold it. We strain our eyes to focus on the light that is coming closer. After a few minutes the light breaks from the trees and takes a turn towards the lake. After another moment it dips and stays in one spot. We then exhale and look at each other.

"Now what?" someone whispers.

"We have to get closer," says Brad as he begins to inch around the bushes. The rest of us inch after him. We crawl on our hands and knees and after about fifteen minutes we stop behind a cluster of headstones and assess the situation. We can see that the light is actually a Coleman lantern placed on a bench. On another bench about twenty feet away sets a hunched figure in a long dark coat with a hood pulled over its head.

A cramp forms in my curled up right leg and silently I straighten it out. When I bring it down again I have the misfortune to set my knee on a twig, a very dry twig that snaps like a gunshot. The figure jumps up, grabs the lantern and shouts, "Who's there?"

With the best of intentions, I am sure, Brian stands up and answers, "Ma'am?"

A scream fills the air and the lantern crashes to the ground, leaving all of us in the dark. Retreating footsteps can be heard and the crush of underbrush.

"Come on. Let's get out of here," says Brad as we all run, tripping over headstones and flowerpots to the lane leading to the main road. We are out of breath as we all try to enter the station wagon via the same door. After much pushing and shoving we find our seats and Brian fishes the keys out of the pocket of his jeans.

"Are we all here?" he asks before he shifts into drive.

"Yes," we all shout. "Lets go!"

At a much faster speed than he used coming to the cemetery, he drives back to his house. It is only after we return the station wagon to the garage and huddle in the tent we discuss what has happened.

"You know who that was don't you?" questions Dan. Most of us shake our heads. "It was Old Miss Calloway! What was she doing there in the middle of the night?"

"Well, she does live right there at Raven Hill, maybe she was out for a walk," suggests Brian.

"Hmmmm. She was sitting there, not walking, and if that is the same light the others have seen, she must go there a lot. I wonder why?" muses Dan.

"Maybe she is visiting her parents," answers Tony.

"No, I know for a fact that they are buried in a fancy mussilini in Grand Rapids. My father took me there once a long time ago," replies Alan.

"You mean a mausoleum?" questions Dan as he rolls his eyes at the younger boy. "But you're right, they are not buried here in Traverse City."

"I guess we had better keep this to ourselves," observes Brian. "Otherwise Mom and Dad would kill me for taking the car out and scaring that woman half to death. Not a word to anyone, right?"

After agreeing to never mention the incident to anyone, the older boys go to the house to sleep, leaving us to fend for ourselves. We drift off to sleep, each deep in thought of what Old Miss Calloway was doing in the cemetery.

For the next few weeks the gossip around town was that a gang of vandals had hit the cemetery and knocked over a few headstones. Rumor also had it that Miss Calloway, investigating the cause of the noise was attacked by one of the hoodlums! Imagine that! What was the world coming to? We seven knew the truth but we didn't dare try and set the record straight, that the headstones were knocked over accidentally in our fright and we never laid a finger on Old Miss Calloway. But we were hardly in a position to defend ourselves.

We just laid low and hoped something would come along and distract the population from that night and toward something else. We didn't have long to wait.

After the holidays, the attention turns toward the Vanneste family and their preparations for the wedding of their only child, the Fair Emily. A date has finally been decided on in the beginning of June and the Old Stone Church has been selected as the site. Speculation has been that the nuptials would take place in Chicago, the hometown of the groom, but Fair Emily has insisted that she wished to me married in her hometown. Only weddings of European Royals capture the imagination of more people than that of our own Fair Emily. She is our town's princess. Beautiful, poised, smart, and sole heir to the Vanneste fortune which is considerable. Amongst the girls in my class, heated discussions broke out about who would be and who wouldn't be invited to the wedding of the century, not that any of them had any say in any aspect of it. When it was announced that kindergartner, Melissa Hoekstra, a distant relative of the Vannestes, was taped to be the flower girl, the dream of every girl in elementary school was dashed.

Activity reaches a crescendo in April, when the invitations of those invited are received. Fights between the invited and not invited girls break out as those with the precious pieces of paper lord it over the others. It is no longer a wedding, it has become the social event of a lifetime, even to pre-teenage girls.

When the engraved envelope arrives at out house, Debbie imme-diately calls Kathy and tells her she just has to come home for that weekend. As for the boys I knew that were invited, we didn't really care that we were, but we did hope the food would be good and no one would mind if we took more than one dessert.

By May, the girls in my class are playing 'Fair Emily's Wedding' in which they practice being guests at the wedding. They practice such things as sitting still, sitting with their legs crossed at the ankles and sitting up straight. Occasionally one pretends to be the bride herself and the others practice greeting her in a mock receiving line. The boys by this time are wondering if they want to get married at all. Those who still wish to, decide on elopement as the only answer.

At home things are not much different. Debbie and Mom spend weekends shopping in different towns for the right dresses. Kathy calls several times to see what they are wearing so she wouldn't clash with them. My good suit will still fit me so all I have to endure is a new tie and shoes. Nope, the town will not soon forget this wedding, and neither will I.

CHAPTER 6

❀

Finally the day of the wedding of Miss Emily Amelia Vanneste and Mr. John 'Jack' Huisjen Van Raalte has arrived. The five members of my family are relaxing over breakfast when the phone call comes. My mother, being closest to the phone, picks up the receiver and after answering with the customary "Hello?" sits transfixed in her chair for a solid two minutes before exclaiming "What! Are you serious Jane?" and then lapsing into rapt silence again.

The rest of us are forced to simply stare at her and quietly whisper, "What? What is it?"

After a few more minutes spent in dying of curiosity, Mom finally says, "Thanks for calling Jane, I think I'll go see what's going on," and hangs up the phone.

Once the phone is returned to its cradle, we can contain ourselves no longer and barrage her with questions. She holds up her hand demanding silence and says, "That was Jane Bartlett. She said that there is a flock of sheep and goats running all over the yard at Oak Lawn."

"Does the wedding have a pastoral theme or something?" asks my puzzled father.

"No, apparently a truck of sheep and goats was parked in front of a restaurant late last night and while the driver was eating the door somehow got open and the animals escaped. It seems they headed for the greenest pastures they could find, which happened to be at the Oak Lawn estate. The driver didn't even realize they were missing until he arrived at his destination early this morning. The Vannestes went to bed early to prepare for the long day and didn't discover them until this morning. I guess they have trampled or eaten everything they could reach. Jane says there is quite a crowd gathered there now."

"Let's go see!" shouts Debbie.

"Oh what's going to happen to the wedding?" frets Kathy.

And with that we all quickly change into jeans and sweatshirts and head out to the car. It only takes five minutes to reach the area of Oak Lawn and discover hundreds of others had the same idea. Dad parks the car in the first spot he can locate on a side street and we all take off at a run to the estate. The scene is utter chaos. People peer over the four-foot high brick wall or climb it and sit along the top of it. We can hear shouting and dogs barking as we draw closer to the estate. Kathy, Debbie and I scramble up the brick wall and stand there to see the action. My mother starts to order us down but stops mid sentence to say, "Honey, give me a hand," and she joins us on the wall. My father is tall enough to have a good enough view from where he stands.

The sight that greets us causes Kathy to exclaim, "Jeez! Look at this place!" and the rest of us to stare in disbelief.

The normally pristine lawn and gardens are in total disarray. Tables and chairs are topsy-turvy and strewn across the lawn. Broken ribbon and garland hang here and there from the bushes and trees or are scattered around on the grass. Running around the great expanse of lawn and trampling what is left of the flowers and greenery is an odd cast of characters. Dozens of sheep, bleating in either anger or panic, I'm not sure which, are darting across the lawn evading being captured by the people or dogs chasing them. A few goats run about as well, but since they have horns that they are shaking at their pursuers, the people and dogs generally leave them alone.

Before my parents can stop them, my sisters jump off the wall and run off in the direction of a small flock of sheep that have been cornered between the wall and a hedge. My mother grabs my arm and says, "Don't you dare, Kevin," (which was unnecessary because joining into the fray had never crossed my mind). A minute later Kathy runs by screaming with a goat in hot pursuit. My mother turns to my father and says, "Tom, why don't you get the girls before they get hurt." While my father goes in search of a gate to pass through, I decide to get another view of the whole situation. After promising my mother not to wander off or get in the way, I jump down and land on the sidewalk and make my way to the front of the mansion.

After I locate an empty spot, I climb the wall and sit down. I look around to see what is happening. I can hear hysterical sobbing and I look up to see the Vanneste family, still dressed in their pajamas and robes standing on the second floor balcony. The hysterical sobbing is coming from Susan Vanneste, the mother of Fair Emily. Her normally perfectly coifed head is disheveled and resting on her only child's shoulder. Emily has her arm around her mother while she surveys the considerable chaos before her with a rather bemused look on her face. Lydia Vanneste stands beside them and is shouting to a man standing below them on the lawn.

"Ray, why aren't your collies herding those sheep?"

"Mrs. Vanneste, I tried to tell you that they were show dogs, they haven't seen a sheep before in their lives."

At that moment two bleating sheep scramble by with a large collie in hot pursuit, looking like she wants to play with them rather than herd them anywhere.

"Get those dogs out of here!" screams the older woman.

Ray shrugs his shoulders and without much enthusiasm he trots in the general direction of the animals that have just run by, calling "Here Laddie, Here Laddie."

Bored with the limited action in the front yard, I make my way back to the back of the house and find my family looking for me.

My father calls to me "Come on Kev. We are going home and getting dressed for the wedding. I'm sure they will tell us then what they are going to do about the reception."

We make our way home and get cleaned up and change into our best clothes while we all muse about what the Vanneste family is going to do about the reception. Our guesses range from the event being held at the park at the lakeshore to the basement of the church.

We leave at noon for the church. The ceremony doesn't start until one and we know getting good seats will be difficult. My sisters want to be there by eleven, but my father puts his foot down on that idea. After parking on a side street blocks from the church we follow the stream of others on the way to the Old Stone Church. We do manage to procure seats about halfway down the aisle on the left side. We are about forty-five minutes early so we have plenty of time to greet friends and neighbors and to look at the lavish floral displays. Baskets of spring flowers decorate the altar area and leafy vines are twisted around columns or are hung from the beams overhead. While my sisters oooh and aah over the décor, I think of how lucky that the sheep hadn't made their way to the church. I notice Miss Calloway seated in the first pew with Emily's family. She is seated at one end of the row while Mrs. Lydia Vanneste is seated all the way on the other side. Just then Mrs. Stockwell leans over the back of our pew and whispers in my mother's ear, "I hear that in exchange for the use of Raven Hill for the reception, Cleary insisted that she be seated in the front row with the family. Is that gutsy or what?"

A string quartet that is sitting off to one side of the sanctuary begins to play a variety of sacred and classical music and also prevents any kind of answer from my mother.

At promptly 1pm the back doors to the sanctuary are slowly opened and the quartet stricks up the traditional wedding march. The congregation stands up and I turn around and strain to see what is happening. The first down the aisle is Melissa, the flower girl and the envy of every girl under ten years of age in town. She smiles happily as she sprinkles rose petals here and there. Next come the bride's maids, five in all. The Maid of Honor is Shari Braun, Emily's friend since childhood; the others I do not recognize and figures they are friends from college or relatives of her soon-to-be-husband. After a slight pause and then a crescendo, the bride appears at the back of the sanctuary. As everyone expected, she is a vision in white lace holding onto her father's arm. They make their way down the long aisle with short deliberate steps. As they pass by where we are sitting I can hear soft oohs and aahs from my sisters. The dress is floor length, with a long train following behind. The lace veil conceals her face and reaches down to her fingertips. In her hands she gently carries a flowing bouquet of pink roses, daisies, and baby's breath. Frank Vanneste finally lets go of his only child when they reach the altar and leaves her at the side of Jack Van Raalte, who has entered, with considerably less fanfare, through a side door while everyone was watching Fair Emily.

The wedding continues for more than an hour, the actual ceremony broken up by a soloist, the church choir, and more music from the quartet. At the end the minister pronounces them husband and wife and when they kiss I can hear my sisters give a deep sigh, which make me roll my eyes for the first time during the ceremony. The couple make their way down the aisle to go and stand on the steps and greet the guests on the way out.

While most of us wait our turn to get in line, Deacon Webster ascends to the podium and announces that the location of the reception has changed from Oak Lawn to Raven Hill. The church erupts in a whispered roar. All around us I can hear comments like "What? Lydia is going *there?*" "Who decided that I wonder?" "That would explain why she was seated with the family" "I hope they can keep those two ladies apart!"

I look at my father and ask him what the trouble is and he merely shakes his head and whispers, "It's nothing," and stands up and ushers his family to the aisle to stand in the reception line. The muted conversations are hard to ignore and my curiosity about Miss Calloway and her big house that I had only seen from a distance is piqued.

Eventually we make our way through the receiving line; I politely shake hands with the parents of the bride and groom, the minister, the members of the wedding party, and a few people none of whom I know. I look for Miss Calloway, but she is nowhere to be seen, probably getting her house ready, I figure.

From the church we go straight home to freshen up for the reception. Debbie and Kathy decide to shed their high heels for something more practical for the lawn reception at Raven Hill. Mom carefully packs the wrapped glass ice tea set that my parents had bought for the married couple in the back seat of the car. My sisters and I had pooled our pittance of savings together and purchased a small crystal candy dish, in remembrance of all the candy she allowed us to eat when she babysat us. Kathy had carefully wrapped the delicate dish in the leftover paper from our parent's gift and tucked the small card into the ribbon tied around it.

Several people had arrived at the reception before us, so we park in the cemetery. My mother gives my father a long look but he quickly speaks up, "There should be a path around here leading to the house." I am just able to catch myself before blurting out that he was right, there is a path, but how could I explain that? We walk in the general direction of the noise and Debbie is the first to shout, "It's here, the path is over here."

After years of peeking through trees from the main road and glimpses from afar from the bay, we three kids are going to see Raven Hill up close. My sisters hurriedly walk ahead of us while I carefully carry the wedding gift. I step out onto the lawn and blink my eyes. Slowly my eyes adjust from the darkness of the woods to the bright sunshine. The great expanse of rolling lawn is teeming with guests and people hired to work the event. Scattered around are canopies, tables, and chairs. My eyes quickly leave the beehive of activity before me and are drawn to the house. It is large, not gigantic as Oak Lawn, not by any means. It is white with hunter green shutters. It stands three stories high with turrets and gables jutting every which way. The wrap- around porch seems to wrap around the entire house and right now the string quartet from the church is playing music on it. I had never seen a house quite like that before in my life. I stand there with my mouth wide open until my mother takes my hand and leads me to a long table piled with gifts and instructs my father and I to place our contributions on it as well. A few of the gifts are already unwrapped and are on display. My mother takes a firm hold of my hand while she examines the display, apparently afraid I might wish to pick something up and play with it. "Oh look, Lydia bought this wonderful set for them," she says to no one in particular as she inspects a punch bowl and piles of small glasses surrounding it. "Ohoooooo. I think it's *Waterford crystal!*" she gasps.

"Knowing Lydia, I'm sure it is," my father replies.

I look over the fine glassware, silver, and linens and look back at my father. "Wow! Wait until they unwrap *all* the gifts."

"I think it will take them several days to unwrap everything. Goodness knows how they will get back to Chicago."

"Do you think they will like our gift?" I ask when I realize the small candy dish pales next to the fine items on the table before me.

My father pats my shoulder. "I know Emily and her new husband will love it because it came from you three." Much comforted I ask for permission to explore the grounds. After receiving the usual warnings about not wondering off or making a nuisance of myself, I set off to explore the estate known as Raven Hill.

I naturally head for the house first. All the doors are open and people are drifting in and out. The rooms are cleared of any small items and most of the furniture pushed against the walls, except for couches and chairs, which are arranged in groupings through the downstairs rooms. Older adults and women with small children take up most of the indoor seating space. The kitchen is humming with the caterers preparing platters and bowls of food and pitchers of drinks. I find a stairway going up and climb them to the second floor. Most of the doors are open and a quick look finds most of them occupied with sleeping babies and toddlers. Bored with being indoors, I make my way back down the stairs and out the nearest door I find. I spy people lining up at a buffet table and get in line. The food is plentiful and I help myself to whatever looks good to me. After filling my plate, I make my way to the lawn where people are eating either at tables or picnic style on the grass. I ignore my sisters, who are with their own friends, and keep walking until I find some of my own school friends sprawled on the grass finishing their own heaped plates of food.

While relaxing in the bright sunshine finishing my meal, I become aware of an overwhelming sweet, floral scent.

"What is that smell?" I ask my friend Pamela. She wrinkles her forehead in thought and answers, "You mean the lilacs? Haven't you smelled lilacs before?"

"Of course I have." And while I had, I had never been so overwhelmed with their scent as I was just then. I look around me and notice large, twisted bushes scattered throughout the lawn. Each branch seems weighed down by the abundance of blossoms.

Pamela interrupts my reverie with the comment; "Don't you know that Raven Hill is the only place in the world with blue lilacs?"

I strain my eyes toward the nearest bush and indeed, the flowers do appear to be a medium blue shade. "You're kidding me. There must be other blue lilacs in the world."

"Nope. Lilacs are only white or shades of violet. This shade of blue is only found here."

"Why is that?"

"No one knows. And if you take a cutting or sucker shoot and plant it somewhere else it will be an ordinary violet color when it blooms. My mom and aunts have tried planting them in their yards and that's what happened," offers Patty, Pamela's older sister.

We spend most of the remaining afternoon looking out over the bay. A large flotilla of boats go by, looking at the spectacle staged above the bluffs. We recognize the boats of some of our friends not invited to the wedding. A few of us walk the lawn and I take the opportunity to get a close up look at the lilac bushes. I pull a branch toward me and bury my face into the blossoms. The smell is wonderful and I can see that they are indeed the color of my faded blue jeans. Frankly I have to admit I didn't know enough about lilacs to say if this is unusual or not.

After my friends are collected one by one by their families, I find my parents in the gazebo talking to Miss Calloway. I approach them quietly and stand next to my father, hoping no one notices me.

Miss Calloway looks at me and interrupts their conversation with "And this must be your son, Kevin, right?"

"It is indeed," answers my father. "Say hello to Miss Calloway."

I say hello and offer my right hand all the while hoping she doesn't recognize me as one of the boys who had scared her so badly the previous fall. She apparently doesn't as she smiles back at me and shakes my offered hand. It is the first time I have a close up look at her and I am surprised. I had expected an old woman, rather like Mrs. Lydia Vanneste, but instead I find someone who, while not young, certainly isn't old. Her dark brown hair is waist length and kept out of her face by a gold clasp. Deep blue eyes are off set by a long linen dress that flows well past her knees. While the adults pick up their conversation, I slip away and head back to the house.

The crowd is thinning and for the first time I notice a brick path leading to a garden next to the house. Curious, I follow the path and hear the tinkling sound of water falling. Vines climbing on wires seemingly create the feeling of being cut off from the rest of the grounds. In the middle of the garden is a large circular fountain. In the center of the fountain are two figures, children, a boy and a girl. They are dressed in raincoats, boots, and wide brimmed rain hats. The girl holds an umbrella over both of them. Water spills from the top of the umbrella and splashes down into the pool at their feet. I am fascinated at the expressive faces of the figures. The girl looks with concern at the smaller boy, who in return seems to stare back with devotion.

I take a seat on one of the benches surrounding the fountain, enjoying peace and quiet for the first time that day. My reverie is short lived, however, as a small group of people filters into the small garden. It is Fair Emily and her family. The young bride smiles and sits next to me, inquiring if I enjoyed the day. I assure her that I had indeed enjoyed the day very much. Her father, mother, and Lydia, her grandmother, sit on another bench while another couple and one of the bridesmaids, who turn out to be the parents and sister of the groom, sit on another bench. Jack, the new groom, enters with a tray of soft drinks and passes them around. There is even enough for me.

"Not trying to steal my girl, are you?" Jack teases as he sits on the other side of Emily.

"Ah, I wish!" I respond.

The group breaks into an easy banter, while I silently relax on my bench, drinking my soft drink. After some time Miss Calloway enters the garden and is greeted by the young couple stating their thanks for the use of her home and grounds. The elder Van Raaltes jump in with more thanks and Emily's parents join in. They are all thanking her except for one, Mrs. Lydia Vanneste. She stands up and without so much as a word walks out of the garden. Quick glances are exchanged between the remaining people, but Miss Calloway acts as if nothing has happened. She takes a seat next to Emily's father and the conversation continues as if nothing has happened.

"While I appreciate having the reception here at Raven Hill, I really wish I could have given you a day that you will always remember," states Susan Vanneste, rather wistfully. Emily tosses back her head and shrieks with laughter. She then puts her hand into Jack's and kisses him on the cheek. "I know I will *always* remember this day, Mom!" The rest of the group is still laughing when my family finally tracks me down and tells me it is time to go home.

More good-byes and thanks are exchanged before we leave. I am exhausted and I fall asleep in the car on the short trip home.

Later, in my own bed, just before I fall asleep again, I wonder why Mrs. Lydia acted that way to Miss Calloway. Didn't she like the house? The yard? Why couldn't she thank her for letting all those people walk all over her house and estate? I decide to talk to my father, certainly if anyone knew, he would.

CHAPTER 7

❀

The sun has been up for hours before I stir from my bed that Sunday morning after Fair Emily's wedding. I make my way down the stairs to find my father and Kathy eating breakfast in the kitchen. I help myself to the cereal and milk on the table and begin to eat although I still feel full from all the food I had eaten the day before. I am also deep in thought about the events of the previous day.

"Good morning Kevin. You seem awfully quiet this morning. Did you sleep well last night?" my father questions me.

"I slept like a rock," I answer truthfully, "Dad, I was just wondering…"

"Yes, Kev?"

"Why does Mrs. Vanneste, ya know the older Mrs. Vanneste, hate Miss Calloway?"

"What makes you say that?"

I relate to him what had happened the day before in the garden at Raven Hill.

"Well, Kev I think hate is too strong of a word to use."

"No, Dad, Kevin is right," Kathy defended me. "The few times I have seen the two of them together, I was glad looks couldn't kill because of the way Lydia Vanneste looks at Miss Calloway. And Miss Calloway just tries to ignore her. It's just weird."

"What are you guys talking about?" asks Debbie as she whisks into the room; showered, dressed and apparently hungry as she makes a quick dive for a clean cereal bowl on the table.

"About Mrs. Vanneste and Miss Calloway," reveals Kathy.

"Agh! They hate each other!"

"See!" Kathy and I say in unison to our father.

"Come on," I beg, "you must know something."

"OK, OK. After we get done eating I'll tell you the story, but this story is not for you to repeat to your friends. Understand?"

The three of us nod excitedly. We have suspected something was between the two women, and now we would finally hear what it was! We finish our cold cereal in record time and then have to wait while our father finishes his and drinks a second cup of coffee. At last he pushes himself away from the table and directs us to the living room where he sits in his comfortable, overstuffed chair and us kids take places on the floor.

"Well," he begins "there are really two stories that explain why there is so much friction between the two of them. I guess I should start with the oldest story first shouldn't I?"

My sisters and I lean forward with excitement.

He begins, "If you happened to notice the furniture in Miss Calloway's house you should know it all came from the Calloway Furniture Company of Grand Rapids."

"Really?" broke in Kathy. "I noticed it looked old and was very elaborate."

He nods, "Yes, that was the style of the time when most of it was made, nearly one hundred years ago. Her great -grandfather was a well-known woodworker in his native England. He came to America and settled in Grand Rapids. He was one of the first to set up a furniture making company there. At one time there were dozens of such businesses in that area."

"He made all that furniture by himself?" a puzzled Debbie asks.

"Oh no. He didn't actually make all of the pieces himself. He would make what you would call a sample and hundreds of workmen would mass-produce the tables, hutches, chairs, and beds. They had a huge showroom and buyers would come from all over the country and order what they wanted to sell in their stores. I believe the furniture at Raven Hill are the sample pieces he produced."

"Is the company still in Grand Rapids?" I ask.

"No. The furniture business pretty much has left the Grand Rapids area and moved elsewhere. The Calloway Company was able to hang on until the death of Cleary's father, Horatio, which was about twenty years ago."

"What does the company have to do with Mrs. Vanneste? Didn't she like their furniture?" broke in Debbie.

My father patiently continues. "It has to do with Mrs. Vanneste coming from a lumbering family. Her grandfather and father owned thousands of acres of pine in western Michigan. She too, comes from a very wealthy family."

"Did the Calloways want the same wood?" I guess.

"No, the Calloways generally used the hardwood trees, you know, like oak trees that grow in southern Michigan and the Vannestes lumbered the soft wood, like pine. But their families knew each other because they were both wealthy and had ties to the Grand Rapids area. It was a widely know fact that Mrs. Vanneste, actually her name then was Lydia Standish, was expected to marry Horatio Calloway. Horatio of course, was the grandson of the founder of the furniture company and was a man with a bright future."

"So why didn't they get married?" demands Kathy.

My father clears his throat and shrugs, "I'm not really sure. Something went awry in their courtship and it was called off. My father, your grandfather, said that the Standish's were dropped like a bad habit by the Calloways and several others who were in their clique."

"But why? What happened?" we all ask.

"I'm not really sure…" Changing the topic he continues "Eventually Horatio met and married the daughter of a newspaperman who ran the local paper here in Traverse City. Her Grandfather had built Raven Hill and they received it as a wedding present. They became the parents of Cleary and Ezra."

"Who's Ezra?" I ask, never having heard the name before.

"He was Cleary's younger brother. He died in Vietnam several years ago."

A thought crosses my mind. "Is he buried in the cemetery near Raven Hill?"

"No, he is buried in the family plot in Grand Rapids. I went to his funeral." My father grows quiet and then adds, "He was the last of her immediate family."

I shrug my shoulders. Obviously, Miss Calloway was not visiting her brother's grave that night we startled her. Perhaps she was just out for a walk after all.

After a short pause, Debbie nudges my father back to the present. "What happened with Lydia?"

"After the shock of the wedding being called off, she traveled and visited various relatives. She also spent several months at the Kellogg Sanitarium and it was there she met Mr. Donald Vanneste, whose family had made their fortune in ship building on the Great Lakes."

"She was in a sanitarium?" shrieked Kathy.

"It wasn't really *that* kind of sanitarium. It was more like what we would call a spa today. The people who went there got plenty of rest and relaxation, not to mention pampering. Most people went there for what they called "nervous conditions" back then. Did you know that it was because of the religious beliefs of Mr. Kellogg that he began to experiment with grains and developed the first breakfast cereals that we still eat today?"

We all shake our heads in unison.

Debbie screws up her face in thought. "After all that they would live in the same town?"

"Well, that was accidental. Raven Hill was a gift from Horatio Calloway's wife's family. Oak Lawn was built by Lydia's grandfather and she inherited the estate after her uncle died some years after she was married. Both the Calloways and Vanneste families traveled extensively or lived in homes in Grand Rapids, so they managed, at least Lydia and Horatio managed not to run into each other very often."

"So, that's the reason they don't like each other? Because Miss Calloway's father wouldn't marry Mrs. Vanneste?"

"Remember when I said this story had two parts?" We all nod. "Well, there is more."

"Let's hear it!" enthused Debbie.

My father resettles himself in the overstuffed chair and continues. "Of course all the young people knew each other back when Traverse City was an even smaller town. So, Cleary and Ezra grew up with Frank and Robert, the sons of Donald and Lydia. They went to school together, played together and eventually Cleary and Frank started dating. The parents, especially Lydia, were not at all happy about that. But time went on and Lydia accepted Cleary as one of the family. They were to be married the summer after Frank graduated from college, but during the Christmas Holidays before the wedding, they called off the wedding. Lydia was furious. She considered it a personal attack on her family and hasn't talked to Cleary since."

"That's it?" asks a disappointed Kathy "I was hoping for something more tragic or scandalous. I notice Frank Vanneste still talks to Miss Calloway."

"For a time it was pretty scandalous. I was in college during that time, but I can remember the called off wedding was a topic of conversation for a long time. And, yes, Frank and Cleary still talk to each other. They have always remained friends, in spite of his mother's feelings," answers my father.

"Dad, why do you call Miss Calloway 'Cleary'?" I ask.

"It was her nickname when she was a kid. Her real name is Clarissa, but her friends always called her Cleary. You knew we grew up together, didn't you?"

"Were you good friends?"

"Oh yes. Their families were a lot wealthier than ours, but we all knew each other from school and church. There was a group of about twenty of us that hung out together. In the summer we would go camping and hiking around the area. In fact, I think I have a picture of us somewhere. Hmmmmm, in fact I just saw it the other week when I was trying to find baby pictures of your Aunt Tina for her 40th birthday party." He got up and walked to the hall closet and pulled out a shoe box and rummaged through it for a few minutes until he found what he wanted. He pulls out a 5x7 photograph in triumph. "I knew I had seen it recently." He sits back down in the overstuffed chair and we gather around to look at the photograph.

"Hey, that's the old Mission Lighthouse," observes Kathy.

"Yes it is," replies our father. "This picture was taken on one of the trips we took up there. We hiked up there at least twice each summer and we would camp near the shore. I doubt we would be allowed to do that today."

I look at the picture of smiling youths arranged in two rows on the beach in front of the familiar lighthouse that stands at the end of the Leelanau peninsula. "Who are these people?"

"Well, in the back row, from left to right we have Carl Frederickson, he lives in Utah now. Mary Jones, she lives in Vermont, Abe Mangum, he lives in Lansing. The next person is Cleary. She would have been seventeen in this picture." Even thirty years later I could easily recognize her. The girl in the photograph is tall, slender, hair down to the top of the jeans she wore. Her youthful face was slightly plumper, but still angular. She was smiling and had one arm around the younger girl standing beside her.

"Who is that next to her?" I ask.

"That is, or should I say was Mariette Beaubien, the daughter of a powerful local politician."

"Was?"

"Yes, she died the summer after this picture was taken from a polio epidemic that hit the area. It was so sad. She was so beautiful with her dark eyes and hair. Lydia Vanneste had her picked out to marry Robert. Yep, Cleary would marry Frank and Robert would marry Mariette. She had dreams of her family 'ruling the town' so to speak, and with Cleary and Mariette in the family she probably would have."

"I thought there was a vaccine for polio," wondered Debbie.

"There is now. But that was still a few years off when this picture was taken, unfortunately."

After a few minutes of silence my father continues with the identification of the persons in the photograph. "Next to Mariette is Frank Vanneste. This would have been the summer before he started college. Now in the first row, we have your Aunt Tina, she was the youngest of the group at age eleven. Then there is me, I was sixteen, and next to me are Ezra, Cleary's brother and Robert, Frank's brother. They would have been twelve along with the girl at the end, Shirley Long, now Shirley Kinney, your friend Tony's mother."

I carefully inspect the occupants of the first row. My Aunt Tina sits cross-legged with her long, blonde hair in braids. Next to her is my father and on the other side of him sits a small, dark haired boy that was Ezra and next to him a lankier, blonde boy that was Robert.

"Isn't Robert dead too?" inquires Kathy.

My father slowly nods. "Yes, both Ezra and Robert are gone, too. They both died in Vietnam. They went into the Airforce together and died a few months apart." My father emits a sad sigh. "I think the shock of Mariette and Robert dying and Cleary calling off the wedding has made Lydia Vanneste the rather bitter woman she is today. I think she takes it out on Cleary because she is the only one still around."

"Why doesn't Miss Calloway just leave?" asks Kathy.

My father shakes his head. "I don't know. But then again, this is her town, too. "

"What was Cleary like? When you were kids?"

"She was outgoing, loved the outdoors. She traveled quite a bit with her parents and brother. She was good in school I remember. Cleary and I would take her parent's small boat out and go fishing in the summer." My father smiles, thinking of his childhood friend. "Yep, the whole gang of us had some good times, but some bad times too. I remember hearing Mariette was ill and then…gone. And around the same time about a dozen of us were involved in a boating accident…"

"Really?" interrupts Debbie.

"About a dozen of us were out boating below the bluffs at Raven Hill when a yacht hit our boat at full speed. The driver it turned out was quite drunk. We were all knocked overboard and were lucky to escape with our lives. Robert was injured the worst. He didn't resurface with the rest of us and we all dove to find him. Cleary found him first and kept his head above water until a boat came along and took him to the hospital. It was touch and go for awhile, but he pulled through. He always said he owed Cleary his life."

"How sad," observes Kathy. "So many of those in the picture died so young."

"Hmmm, yea," agrees Debbie "So, Lydia Vanneste can't stand Cleary because she didn't marry her son, although she did save the life of the other son and things didn't turn out the way she expected. I guess it sort of makes sense."

I nod my head. It *did* make sense, but as my sisters get up from the floor in search of something else to do, I lean back on my elbows, deep in thought. Perhaps it was the whole story, but perhaps not.

CHAPTER 8

With the wedding of Fair Emily and Jack Van Raalte over, life falls back into its usual routine. The rest of the summer is spent playing with friends and taking turns camping in each other's back yards. I yearn to go hiking and camping further afield as my father had done with his friends, but the answer is always the same: "You're too young. Things were different in the 40's and 50's than they are now in the 80's. When you get to be sixteen or so we will talk." When you are ten, sixteen seems a long way off, so my friends and I are forced to content ourselves with camping close to home.

That fall I enter fifth grade and my attention turns to my school-work and playing pick-up football games with my friends in the neighborhood. I never give the Calloway or Vanneste families a thought until late in November when I accept a ride to the library with my sister Debbie.

Debbie has finally passed her driver's test and uses any excuse to drive the family Buick, the result being that she offers me a ride to the library nearly every day. As it happens I have a paper due on the American buffalo, so I am happy to accept when she loudly (in front of our parents) offers to drive me to the library on a rainy Saturday morning. As we near the library, I cringe when I realize she is going to attempt to parallel park on the street. But after only five tries she manages to park only a foot away from the curb. With relief I climb out of the car and we make our way inside. I head for the children's room and Debbie heads for the Romance reading section.

After selecting a few volumes I set out for the checkout counter. As I pass by a support pillar I notice a large photograph had been hung there that hadn't been there on previous visits. It shows the celebration in the streets of Traverse City after it was announced World War II was over. I recognize it as a photograph that had been in the exhibit I had seen a little over a year ago. I hear someone come up behind me to see Mrs. Morris, one of the librarians, admiring the photograph with me.

"I saw that picture last year, at the old photography studio," I inform her.

"Yes," she smiles. "It's one of them. The photographs were donated to the library and they will be displayed every now and then."

A thought crosses my mind. "Where is the one with the girl on the train?"

Mrs. Morris purses her lips and then replies, "The one with the girl skipping rope?"

I nod my head.

"It's funny you should ask that." She then leans over and in a conspiratorial whisper adds, "Last month, when the pictures arrived, we noticed that we had received 49 photographs instead of the expected 50. Our Director brought it to the attention of the Library Board. She got a letter stating that one of the photographs had been sold and no one was to ask any more questions about the missing photo. We thought it was so strange. We guessed the missing photograph was that of the girl skipping rope on top of the train car. It was a nice picture, but why not just have a copy made?" she muses. "Well, I must get back to my desk," she adds as she hurries off.

I am disappointed that I won't see my favorite picture from the exhibit, but wasn't it curious it had disappeared? I realize it is getting late and I had better find my sister before she comes to look for me.

As it turns out she is looking through the paperbacks when I find her and announce that I am ready to leave.

"I'm almost done, just give me a few more minutes."

Not really in a hurry to go home, I wander around the bookshelves in the adult nonfiction section. Hearing angry voices I step behind a unit of books and peek through to the other side. Being rather short, all I can see are waists of two women. The waist closer to me belongs to the older, shorter, and chubbier of the two and I can tell she is doing most of the talking. The older person's arms are waving in the air as if emphasizing what she is saying.

"You can put those books right back on those shelves. You won't have any need of them," the older woman is saying.

"I am just making a gift. There can't be anything wrong with that. Can there?" replies the other woman, who is taller and much more slender.

"We don't need anything from you. You have done enough to my family." With those words she walks past the end of my shelf of books. It is Mrs. Lydia Vanneste. She walks so fast and determinedly that she never glances my way to see me cringing against the row of books behind me. I take a deep breath and walk around the bookshelf to see who she is talking to. It is not a surprise to find Miss Calloway standing there, looking like she is about to cry. In her hands she holds a half dozen books with such titles as *Sewing for Children* and *Knitting Adorable Baby Clothes*.

For some reason I feel like I have to say something to the upset woman in front of me. "Hi Miss Calloway. So nice to see you again." I force a wide smile.

She looks up in surprise and gives me a sad smile in reply. "Why hello Kevin. Nice to see you again too. I don't suppose your father is with you?"

She looks like she needs someone to talk to and it isn't a ten-year-old boy. "No, I came with Debbie, my sister. She has her license now. Scary huh?"

She smiles again and wipes her eyes with the back of her hand.

"I must find my sister now."

"Yes, of course. Take care Kevin."

After Debbie and I are safely on our way home I tell her about the discussion I had overheard.

"Wow! What was Miss Calloway making that would upset the old lady so much?" muses Debbie.

I feel I should tell Debbie that she should not call Lydia Vanneste an "old lady", but I don't feel up to it at this moment. I do speak up with, "She was looking at books that told how to make baby clothes."

With that news, Debbie squeals and nearly runs us off into a ditch.

"What's wrong with you?"

"Geez Kev, you don't suppose Emily is going to have a baby do you?"

I shrug my shoulders. "I'm sure Miss Calloway knows a lot of people having babies."

"Well, I guess we will find out soon."

     ❈   ❈   ❈

It would be a week later in school when that question would be answered. During a math exercise I can hear a few of the girls giggling and talking. "Hey! Can't you girls be quiet?" I scold.

One of them, a chatty girl named Julie, leans toward me and states, "We are guessing what she is going to call the baby."

I raise an eyebrow toward our teacher, Mrs. Carson. She seems a little old to be having a baby, I thought.

Julie, seeing me eye Mrs. Carson, laughs out loud.

"Children! Please be quiet," requests Mrs. Carson.

"Not *her*," she snickered, "Emily."

"Emily?" I ask numbly.

"Emily. You know, Fair Emily. She is having a baby in the spring. We think she should be called either Guenevere or Victoria."

"Noooooo. She should be called Elizabeth or Isabella!" interrupts Sandy.

"And if it's a boy?" I inquire.

Julie, along with the other girls at the table, screws up her face as if the mere mention of her having a boy is just too horrible to think about. "We think she should have a girl, at least for her first baby." And with that she flips her hair over her shoulder and finally gets down to business on her math problems.

I sit in stunned silence. So Emily is having a baby and Emily is the recipient of the gift that the two women were fighting about. But just because Miss Calloway didn't marry her son, why does it mean that she can't make a gift for her son's grandchild? Well, anyway, I am happy Emily is having a baby, but I hope it will be a boy and Kevin would be a good name.

CHAPTER 9

It is with great glee that I set my book bag down by my bed and kick it under my bed. Christmas break has finally arrived and I am looking forward to two whole weeks of fun and freedom. It is supposed to be a routine holiday season and it at least starts out that way. Kathy comes home from college, sporting a new hairstyle and about 10 extra pounds. On the weekend before Christmas Day we make our annual trip to Detroit to visit my grandparents on my mom's side and her only sibling, Aunt Mary. Aunt Mary was married to Uncle Henry and they are the parents of my four cousins that range in age from six to fifteen.

The rest of the time is spent playing and sledding with my friends. Of course we are invited to a few holiday parties, the most sought after invitation being to the annual Christmas Eve party at Mrs. Vanneste's estate, Oak Lawn.

Actually the word 'party' doesn't quite describe the yearly extravaganza that goes on at Oak Lawn each Yuletide. On the outside of the house each evergreen is draped with dozens of strings of bright white lights. Luminaries light the driveway and the two walkways to the house. On the East lawn of the house a painted, hand carved, life-sized twenty-piece nativity scene sprawls over the great expanse. On the West lawn, an entire life sized choir is poised as if singing a holiday tune. Not only is there a choir, but a director and soloist are also included. At night both the nativity and choir are lit up with a whole series of spotlights. The house itself is covered with evergreen swags and red ribbons. A wood and fabric star illuminated with several light bulbs tops the highest chimney. More than once this star was mistaken for the control tower at the local airport.

The only thing more decorated than the outside is the inside of Oak Lawn. A lighted and decorated Christmas tree is on display in every room. Evergreen swags, tied with red ribbons are hung from the ceilings, fireplace mantles, and the staircases. Tables that hold the food are set with the finest linen and silver. Instead of the normal paper plates, we would pile our food on china plates. Granted, these plates are the survivors of past china collections used by the Vannestes, but the plates are china none-the-less. The only exception to the exquisite taste displayed by the hosts is the plastic cups from which the children drink their soda and juice.

Only the first floor is used for the party, but people would sneak up one of the stairways to the second floor and it proved to be just as overdone as the first. I had never gone up to the third floor, but maybe this year.

We enter through the front door where a young woman in a maid's uniform and an older man in a suit and tie greet us. They take our hats and coats from us and hang them on a mobile coat rack that when full, is rolled into one of the walk-in closets and another empty coat rack wheeled out in its place.

After leaving the foyer, my sisters take off in one direction and I in the opposite with my mother's admonishment to behave ourselves. I decide to start at the west end of the house and work my way east. The most western rooms are the library and music room. Stiff leather bound books line shelves that reach from the floor to the tall ceiling. A wooden ladder on wheels could be moved when one wanted a book off the top shelves. Leather chairs are situated in front of a small fireplace and a large braided rug covers most of the parquet flooring. While the library is dark and rather stuffy, the music room is bright and airy. Windows line the two outside walls. Glass French doors lead from the music room to the main living room. A grand piano and an ancient harpsichord are the only musical instruments in residence, making the large room look even larger.

I pass through the glass French doors into what is used as the main living room. This is packed with most of the guests, who either stand around in small groups or sit on one of the many chairs or couches scattered around. One wall is taken up with a huge stone fireplace. If there wasn't a fire blazing in the massive hearth, I could have easily stood up inside. Continuing on my journey and heading north, I enter the dining room. Matching chairs surround a table that can seat twenty. The sliding leaded glass doors are retracted back into the walls, making the dining room an appendage of the living room. The table is covered with linen and an extravagant evergreen and flower display graces the center of the table. I'm sure Mrs. Vanneste is expecting guests might wish to eat at the table, but few dared risk marring the finish of the polished wood even if it is covered with linen.

If one continues west from the dining room, you find yourself in the kitchen. I decide to avoid the hustle and bustle of the crew of caterers and weave through the crowd in the living room instead, and come to the foyer from which I had entered the house earlier. Crossing the foyer I enter another living area as large as the previous living room. Instead of the dining room to the north, this room holds the grand staircase. The stairs go up halfway and then divide, so one is forced to go either right or left. The banisters are hand carved into ornate designs. They are also large, sturdy, and are great fun to slide down. This I know from past experience. As soon as guests begin to leave and fewer people are about, the children sneak off to the staircase and take turns sliding down. But right now there are too many people about to try that. Maybe later. I walk past the staircase and make my way through another crowd of people in that room. At the end of the room is a hallway that leads west for a few yards and then takes a sharp right turn. This hallway holds the bathrooms and storage rooms off to the right and to the left is my favorite room of all.

The East sitting room, much like the music room, is lined with windows, with a large fireplace at one end. It is this room that holds the fascination of many of the children in attendance. Paintings of British hunt scenes cover the walls and the furniture consists of overstuffed leather chairs and couches. It is the East sitting room where the refreshments are offered under the close watch of Earl, Mrs. Vanneste's butler. We kids are only allowed the soft drinks, juice and non-alcoholic punch, but once we get our drinks we wander over to a table set up in front of the French doors leading to the gardens. On it is placed a tower of delicate glasses. At 4:00pm sharp a crowd would gather, Earl would climb a stepladder, and someone would hand him a bottle of champagne. With a sharp 'pop' the cork would fly through the air and bounce off the far wall. He would then tip the bottle and the liquid would flow into the glasses below. When that bottle was empty, someone would hand him another and another cork would explode into the air. This would continue until all of the glasses were full. Then Earl would hand full glasses down to outstretched hands below him. I was always amazed that never a drop spilled onto the crisp white linen on the table.

After asking for a plastic cup of my favorite soft drink, I leave the room via the far door. I am back to the hallway, but instead of retracing my steps I cross the hall and push open a swinging door in front of me and find myself in the back foyer. Located there are the back stairs, much smaller and plainer than the grand staircase. It is there that I find my friends, Ted and Pamela, sitting on the back staircase. I go to join them and it is there that I get my first meeting of Fair Emily since her wedding. She opens the little door that leads from the kitchen to the foyer which in turn leads to the stairs we are sitting on. At first she is startled to see someone, but when she realizes who we are she smiles and greets us by name. She looks slightly pudgy with a definite bulge in her midriff. A minute later her husband, Jack, steps quietly out of the kitchen, the gentle twinkling sound of glass hitting glass can be heard from the wicker basket that he carries.

"Come dear, we must hurry," he whispers.

With a quick smile to us, she whispers, "Now don't tell anyone you saw us. Please?"

"Sure," we all answer in unison. With that the young couple turns and walks out into the cold and blowing snow.

"I wonder where they are going?" muses Pamela.

Before we can discuss the matter further, Mrs. Lydia Vanneste walks into the foyer from the hall. Spying us she asks, "Have you seen Emily?"

We quickly look at each other and with perfectly straight faces answer, "No, we haven't seen her."

"Hmmmmp! Where is that girl? Well, I'm sure she will show up. " Looking back at us she orders, "You kids get out and join the party. I didn't pay all this money to have people to sit on the stairs."

"Yes Ma'am," we answer. Just then Emily's mother comes out of the kitchen and nearly drops the pie she is carrying when she sees the elder Mrs. Vanneste.

"Hungry Susan? Have you seen your daughter? She seems to have disappeared."

"No, no," she stammers. "I think she may have gone for a walk to get some fresh air. I think the smell of the food was making her ill. You must remember what it's like in her…ah…condition," she finishes awkwardly with a glance toward us.

The elder woman merely nods and walks back toward the hall. The younger Mrs. Vanneste breathes a sigh of relief and looks at us still standing on the stairs. "Did Emily leave already?"

Pamela speaks up. "Yes, just before Mrs. Vanneste came into the room."

"Good," is all that she replies and she goes back into the kitchen carrying the pie.

"Well, that was weird!" exclaims Ted.

"Sure was," I quickly agree.

"I don't feel like going back to the party, " states Pamela "Let's look around on the third floor."

"I hear its haunted by the dead Mr. Vanneste," adds Ted.

"Which one? The old lady's husband or her son?" questions Pamela. "You know their younger son died in Vietnam a long time ago."

"I meant the old one. He died in this house you know. His son died far away, how could he haunt this place?"

"He died over there, but he is buried near here in Traverse City. I bet he visits."

I am quickly tiring of this conversation. "Let's go if we are going to look around on the third floor."

We ascend the stairs and pass the landing to the second floor. The next flight of stairs is narrow and unlit. In the gloom I slip and bang against the wall. A framed photograph falls from the wall and lands next to me with a dull thud.

"Geez, I hope I didn't break anything!" I doubted if I could afford to replace any item found in this mansion. I bend down and pick it up. I didn' t hear the tell tale sound of broken glass, but just to be sure I carry it with me to the top of the stairs and into the narrow hallway of the third floor. Ted flicks on the light switch and the three of us anxiously look at the photograph. It is a family picture and judging by their outdated clothing, it was taken decades ago. A set of parents sit stiffly on a set of chairs with a lone child sitting before them on a low ottoman in the center of the photograph. The child is a blonde girl with a large bow tied at the nap of her neck. She stares, almost defiantly, out of the picture.

"You know, it looks like Emily," comments Pamela.

I look at the girl more closely and indeed she does look a lot like Emily, or should I say, Emily looks like her. Before I could say she was right, Pamela adds, "Oh my gosh! It's Mrs. Vanneste! It's hard to think she was ever a kid like us."

"Yea, but she still has that look on her face," comments Ted. We laugh. "Come on, let's look around and then we can hang it back on the way down."

We take a quick tour of the third floor. Much to our disappointment it consists of two communal bathrooms and four suites that each consists of a bedroom and sitting room for the live-in staff, only two of which are occupied. We make our exit down the same staircase that we came up and replace the picture on the wall.

When we hit the main floor we scatter to find our own families. I find my father talking to the Bleichers, our neighbors. I tug on his sleeve to get his attention. He turns to me. "Why hello, Kev. Your Mother has been looking for you."

"Can I talk to you?"

"Sure." He excused himself from the neighbors.

I pull him to an empty corner of the room and whisper, "I saw a picture of Mrs. Vanneste as a little girl. Is she the same girl in the picture that we saw at the exhibit? You know, the girl on the train?"

My father gave me a surprised look. "Yes Kevin, I believe that was her."

"But…"

"Don't say anything now. I'll tell you the story when we get home tonight. OK?"

I nod and feeling hungry find my way to one of the linen covered tables that are set up in all of the rooms and help myself to some of the delicacies that are piled on various platters. After filling my plate, I rejoin Ted and Pamela and other friends in the music room where we spend the rest of the afternoon.

We leave the party soon after darkness falls and head home to freshen up for Christmas Eve services at the Old Stone Church. At the service we are seated near the front, a few rows behind the Vanneste family. I notice that Fair Emily would turn her head and look at the congregation, as if looking for someone.

Later that night, as my father comes in to tuck me in, I remind him of his promise to tell me the story of Mrs. Vanneste and the picture.

He smiles and clears his throat and leans back in the chair next to my bed. "Well, it's hard to believe, but Lydia, Mrs. Vanneste, used to be a girl, and a rather wild one at that. I didn't tell you the whole story before, but understand you are not to talk about this with your friends. There are still people around who could be hurt if all of this was dug up again."

I nod in agreement.

"As a child she would follow her parents as they traveled around inspecting their logging operations. I hear she would play around the trains parked on the sidings that were used to haul the lumber to mills. Sometimes she would stay on the trains when they started moving and would be miles away before someone realized she was missing. Then of course they had to track her down. Her parents weren't too amused to say the least. She was sent to boarding school and promptly ran away. When she was in her mid teens her parents began to live at Oak Lawn, hoping a stable life would calm her down. They also had their sights on young Horatio Calloway, the heir to the furniture company I told you about. They would visit Grand Rapids often to partake in the social life it offered and invited the Calloways to visit at least a few times a year. Things went well for a few years, but Lydia's past caught up to her eventually and the Calloways were shocked with her behavior. Even though it had all happened years before, the Calloways cut off the friendship between the families and as they say 'that was that.' Horatio eventually met Anne and married her."

"Despairing that anyone would marry a girl with such a wild past, Lydia had become despondent, and her family sent her to stay with a distant relative. Sadly, the relative died in a tragic explosion and

Lydia entered the Kellogg Sanitarium for what they referred to in those days as 'nerves' and was prescribed peace and quiet. That's where she met her future husband, Donald Vanneste."

"So it was because she was such a wild girl she wasn't allowed to marry Horatio? That's pretty mean." I suddenly felt sorry for the old lady.

My father shrugged his shoulders. "Times were different. I'm not sure they would have married anyway. They were not engaged. Who knows? They may have married other people eventually anyway. But I think the public humiliation was the worst for Lydia."

"Is that the real reason she hates Miss Calloway? Not just because she didn't marry her son?"

"Well, I think it was a combination of the two things. Her not marrying the man of her parents' dreams and then the daughter of that man calling off the wedding to her own son. It must have raised the old wounds of the past. But I don't know, there seems to be something else."

"Like what?"

"I don't know. There just seems to be something else. Anyway, it's getting late and tomorrow is Christmas. Good night and sweet dreams, Kevin."

With that I fall asleep thinking the mystery is solved. Little did I know it was just beginning.

CHAPTER 10

The joy of the holidays continues for another week, until New Year's Day 1981 to be exact. That morning at 6 A.M. the jarring sound of a telephone ringing wakes me out of my deep sleep that I had only started four hours before. I lay in my bed quietly, straining to hear my father's low voice as he talks to the unknown person on the phone. In a minute my father's voice stops and I can hear my mother talking in higher tones. While I can't hear the words, I can tell she is very upset. Her voice soon stops only to be replaced by the sounds of her feet hitting the floor and drawers being opened and shut.

I quickly pull the covers off me and walk to their room. I stand in the doorway, watching my mother scurry between the dresser, the closet; back to the bed, on which she flings clothing, shoes and other items. My father is sitting silently on the edge of the bed, also watching her.

"What's going on?"

Only my father turns at the sound of my voice. "We got a phone call from Grandma Turner. It seems your Grandparents, Uncle Henry and Aunt Mary and the kids were coming home from a party and were hit by a drunk driver."

"Are they OK?"

"Well, except for the youngest two who were in car seats and Grandma, they were all hurt pretty bad. Your mom is going to Detroit to look after things for awhile."

In the space of an hour my mom is packed, showered, and on her way to Detroit. After she leaves we all sit glumly down to breakfast. We have barely finished when the phone rings. Thinking it is news from Detroit, we let dad answer it while we pick up the dishes.

"WHAT!?"

At that, all of our attention is turned toward our visibly upset father holding the receiver up to his ear.

"Is it Uncle Henry and Aunt Mary?" we ask in unison.

He shakes his head and then says, "Could you guys go and watch TV for now?" We just set down the dishes on the counter and leave the room.

About a half-hour later our father comes into the living room with disbelief on his face. "I guess we all need to have a talk right now. I just got off the phone with my boss. It seems that the accountant at the Grand Rapids store has run off with the store's money. They want me to go and straighten out the books and figure out how much is missing. I might be gone for several weeks."

"You mean he embezzled?" Kathy asked.

"I'm glad that money isn't going to waste sending you to college," he teased. Sobering up, "What am I going to do with you two?" He looks at Debbie and me. "I don't have to leave until Sunday, so I have four days to figure out something."

"We can stay here."

"I could take this semester off."

"No! You're not doing that. I can figure out something." Looking at his watch he adds, "I guess I'll start calling around in a few more hours."

By the end of the day things are decided, but not to my liking. Kathy of course, will go back to school for the next semester. Debbie will go stay with her friend Missy. Both girls have been cast in the high school's spring production of "South Pacific" so it is felt that this way they can attend play practice together. Debbie is thrilled at this news, as she had been afraid that she would have to drop out of the musical. Another plus is that Missy is an only child and her parents will welcome that chance to have Debbie come and stay.

After telling Debbie her good news he turns to me. "I didn't think any of your friends' parents were in a position to take in a ten year old boy for several weeks, so I called an old friend who said she would be willing. You're going to stay with Miss Calloway."

Well, he could have knocked me over with a feather after telling me that. I am in shock. He is sending me off to live with the town oddball. "You have to be kidding!" is my response.

"No, I'm not. Cleary is a very nice woman. I expect you to behave yourself and be nice to her." And that ends the conversation.

The night before I am to go to Miss Calloway's, I pack up my clothes and school supplies. Debbie and Kathy come by my room to cheer me up.

"Come on, Kevin, cheer up. I'm sure I'll see you on the weekends. Maybe we can come home and spend the night every once in a while."

"No. You'll be happy at Missy's house; you'll just ignore me. Just like you always do."

"Hey, I like Missy, but I'm sure I'll need a break from her once in awhile. I promise to see you at least once a week. Really."

I just roll my eyes.

Kathy speaks up. "She can't be that strange. Dad likes her. Known her all his life."

I look up at the ceiling. I'm still not thrilled. "Well maybe staying there won't be too bad. She does live in a nice house."

"She sure does!" Kathy exclaims. "This is a great opportunity to live in a really fancy house. Not like this cracker box we live in. She has a housekeeper, so you probably can be as messy as you want."

Debbie snorts "Don't be like *her.* My room is only clean when she is at school."

"*Your* room?"

I can tell another fight is on its way. "OK, OK, I feel better. Now let me pack." I watch them leave, thinking I can't believe I am going to miss *that.*

The next morning we load up the car with all of our suitcases. Debbie is dropped off first. Next we drive out to the Leewanau Peninsula and turn into the winding driveway of Raven Hill.

"WOW! I think it looks even bigger in the winter," comments Kathy from the passenger seat.

It isn't until I shut the car door and look at the house while Dad pulls my two suitcases and duffel bag from the trunk and places them on the driveway. After shutting the trunk, he hands me the lighter suitcase and we walk up the shoveled walkway to the kitchen door. The light is on and we can see someone moving around inside. My dad knocks softly and the form moves to the door. It opens to reveal an older, dark haired woman.

"Hello, Rose."

"Why hello, Thomas." Smiling at me she adds "Kevin."

A door opens into the kitchen and there she is in the flesh. Old Miss Calloway. She looks at my dad. "I was so sorry to hear about Laura's family. I hope they recover soon."

"I do too. It looks like they will all recover eventually. We were lucky in that respect. Now if I can straighten out those books."

"I'm sure you will. But Kevin is welcome here in the meantime. Your daughters are also welcome, too."

"Kathy is on her way back to college, but I'm sure Debbie will need some time off from her friend and them from her, I'm sure."

Miss Calloway laughs. My dad hands her a piece of paper. "Here are everyone's phone numbers in case you need to get a hold of us." With that he gives my shoulder one last squeeze and he walks out the door. He still has to drive Kathy to school and then back to Grand Rapids in order to start his work the next day.

I just stand there, numbly staring at these two women.

"Thank you for taking me in, Miss Calloway."

"That sounds so formal. Just call me Cleary. Everyone does."

"And call me Rose," the older woman adds.

Cleary picks up the suitcase; Rose picks up the duffel bag. "Come on, I'll show you to your room."

I pick up the other suitcase and follow the two women through the kitchen door and climb the stairs to the second floor. Just as we reach the top of the stairs, they turn right and walk into a bedroom. They place the duffel bag and suitcase on top of one of the twin beds and turn towards me. "Kevin, we'll leave you alone to unpack. The bathroom across the hall is yours, so feel free to leave your toiletries in there. When you're done, come back downstairs and we'll have lunch." With that they file out the door and go back downstairs, leaving me alone.

I look around at my new surroundings. Two twin beds are set parallel to each other, one under the window that looks out over the bay. I decide to sleep on that one. Next to the bed is a small nightstand with a ticking clock and lamp placed upon it. On the other side of the nightstand is the other twin bed that is covered with my luggage. I open one of the suitcases and lift out my underwear and socks first. I decide to put them in the chest of drawers that stands at the foot of the bed that I have decided to sleep in. I pull out one of the drawers and notice an old, faded sticker on the inside of the drawer. I look closer and read the words "Calloway Furniture Company, Grand Rapids, Michigan."

The few hanging items I own are placed in the small closet that I locate opposite the foot of the other twin bed. I walk across the hall and open the door to the bathroom. The tub is unlike anything I have ever seen before. The white ceramic sides are so tall that I wonder how I will ever be able to lift my legs high enough to step in it.

On each corner of the tub are golden feet that look like they might belong to a raven, if of course, the raven was four foot high. A light is over the mirror that is placed over the sink and the vanity. I place the few toiletries that a ten-year-old boy owns on the top of the vanity and squaring my shoulders, I nervously make my way downstairs.

CHAPTER 11

The alarm clock seems to explode in my ear. I fumble in the darkness to locate the source of the racket. I pick up the small, vibrating clock and push in the small button in the back. I set up in bed and swing my feet to the floor. I set there for a moment in the dark silence and orient myself to my new surroundings. After setting the clock down on the nightstand I switch on the lamp. The day before Cleary had told me that either she or Rose would be up to make me breakfast and drive me to school. I look at the clock and it tells me that it is 6:15. I don't hear anyone else stirring in the house, so I decide to shower and dress before venturing downstairs.

Twenty minutes later I quietly make my way down the stairs and see a light under the door leading to the kitchen. I slowly push open the door to find Rose standing over a large pot on the stove. Hearing the door open, she turns around and seeing me smiles "Good morning, Kevin. The oatmeal is almost ready. If you'll sit down, I'll go ahead and pour you some orange juice."

I make my way over to the small kitchen table that is already set with bowls, silverware, and glasses. She pours me a tall glass of orange juice before resuming her vigil over the pot on the stove.

There is shuffling at the kitchen door before it is opened, revealing Mr. Griekos, Rose's husband.

"My heavens Sal, close the door, you're letting in the cold."

He merely grins as he shuts the door and I have the feeling he has heard the same command before. "Good morning, Kev. Sleep OK?"

"Yes, sir."

He sits down next to me and pours himself a glass of orange juice. "It sure is nice to have a young person in the house again.'

"Again?"

"Why yes. Rose and I practically raised Miss Clarissa and her brother Ezra." A shadow crosses his face. "You may not know she had a brother who died in Vietnam."

"Oh, yes. My dad told me."

"Of course, I forgot who your father is. It's hard to keep track of who knows what in this town."

Rose shoots him a look over the pot she is carrying to the table. She sets the pot on the table and starts ladling heaping portions into three of the four bowls on the table. "It's so nice to have someone new to cook for. Not that I don't enjoy cooking for Sal and Cleary, but it's great to have company. We haven't had company since…"

Now it is Mr. Grieko's turn to give Rose a *look*.

My curiosity is short lived as just then the door swings open to reveal Cleary standing there. She is dressed in old jeans and an over-sized University of Michigan sweatshirt. While she is dressed, it is obvious that she hasn't taken any more steps toward being ready to leave the house. "I am so sorry! I'm not used to getting up before dawn. Can you tell?" she laughs.

"Have some breakfast Cleary," chides Rose.

"No. I'll finish getting ready and take Kevin to school and then eat. With that she turns and we can hear her running up the stairs.

I finish the bowl of oatmeal; I even scrape the bottom of the bowl. I am surprised to find that I actually like oatmeal, at least how Rose prepares it. I don't have the heart to tell her that she doesn't really need to go through all the trouble; I am used to a bowl of cold cereal in the mornings.

After we finish breakfast and I gather up my schoolbooks, Cleary comes down the stairs, still dressed as she was before, but with her hair combed and her face washed. She then walks out to the garage and pulls an ancient station wagon around to the house and gently blows the horn.

I pull on my boots and Mr. Griekos hands me my book bag. "We'll see you this afternoon after school."

I nod and walk out the door and get into the passenger's seat of the station wagon and Cleary waits until I buckle my seat belt before putting it into gear and starting down the driveway. "I must warn you that if we get a large snow fall, it may take Mr. Griekos a while to plow the driveway. You may be late to school. I guess I should go to the principal's office and tell them that you're staying with me. I doubt your father had a chance to since the school was closed over the holidays."

"Yes…no. I mean, I know he didn't call. I guess I should also tell you that next week are parent-teacher conferences. I don't think either mom or dad will be able to come to that."

"I'll ask about that this morning. You are a good student, aren't you Kev? I'm not going to receive a horrible surprise if I come to the conference am I?"

It never occurs to me that she might be teasing me. I sit silently, thinking of my recent transgressions. "Well, I did pull Pam's hair a few weeks ago."

Cleary laughs as she parks the car next to my elementary school. "I'm sure the teacher will give me a positive evaluation of your behavior. I'm sure you're just like your father." We walk toward the entrance and find my friends Ted and Tony waiting for me. I had told them about my living with Cleary while my parents are gone, but nonetheless they stare at Cleary with their mouths open. Cleary pretends not to notice and we keep on walking into the building and head toward the principal's office.

I stand next to Cleary as she explains to the principal that I will be staying with her for the next few weeks and giving him her phone number and address. She goes on to ask if she can take my parents' place next week at the conferences. He assures her that it will be fine and she seems to be happy to attend them. With that done, we leave the office and find Ted and Tony waiting for us with looks of sympathy on their faces. Cleary puts her hand on my shoulder and says that she will come and pick me up after school at 3 o'clock. I say goodbye and watch her leave the building.

"Well? What is it like living at Raven Hill with Old Miss Calloway?" Tony finally blurts out.

"It's fine. She is very nice and so are the Griekos."

Just then Anne and Barb, two girls from my class, run up to me and inquire what I am doing with Old Miss Calloway.

I quickly explain about my parents' situations and Cleary is kind enough to take me in for a few weeks.

"Wow! My brother Paul told me that Debbie is staying with Missy and you are out at Raven Hill, but I didn't believe him. Does she wander the house in a long white dress with a candle? I heard she does! Is she really weird? I heard she rarely leaves that house."

Clutching my fists I look Anne squarely in the eye. "Look here, Miss Calloway drove me here today, so she does leave the house. And she was nice to take me in on such short notice."

"Hrrrummp!" Anne replies as she turns and walks away. I am relieved that she has left, as I am afraid to address the question of Cleary being weird. She is obviously a different type of person. And where did that story of her wandering the house in a white dress come from? She isn't a ghost!

The rest of the school day goes on much the same way. It seems everyone knows that I am living with the town eccentric. It is with much relief that the dismissal bell rings and I gather my belongings together and walk out the door with Tony and Ted who then head toward the school bus I normally take with them. I look around and find Cleary standing in the parking lot next to the station wagon. She waves at me to get my attention. Did she really have to do that? I mean, it is bad enough everyone knows I am living with her. Now it looks like she really enjoys having me living with her. I trot off in her direction and get quickly into the station wagon, shutting the door. She doesn't seem to notice that I am in a hurry to get out of the school area and takes her time getting into the car and inquires about my day. I volunteer the basics of how my day had gone but I decide to leave out the comments from my friends.

Later that evening, I set the book I am reading for school aside and get ready for bed. I am still stuffed from the delicious supper that Rose had prepared and exhausted from laughing while the four of us played such card games as Kings-on-the-Corner and Oh Hell, which Mr. Griekos suggested I call Oh Heck if I played with my friends and family. I turn off the lamp and draw the covers over me. If all I have to deal with is good cooking and fun games, then the other kids can think whatever they want to.

CHAPTER 12

The first week back to school goes by quickly. Before I know it, Cleary is picking me up in the station wagon and I am struck by the realization that I have two whole days ahead of me alone with her and the Griekos. As if reading my mind, Cleary turns to me. "I'm sorry Kevin, I was hoping we could do something fun this weekend, but tomorrow I have to go to Grand Rapids to meet with someone who is planning an exhibit about furniture making in Grand Rapids this summer. I said I would help long before I found out I would be keeping you for a while."

"That's OK. I don't want to be in the way, Cleary."

"Well, there is more. The Griekos are also going to be gone to a family gathering. They will probably be gone all day. I was going to have you stay with your sister but then I realized that the plumber is coming over and I had to wait four weeks to get this appointment. Would you mind staying at Raven Hill and letting him in?"

"Oh no. I don't mind." And I didn't, in fact, I was happy to be able to make myself useful. I was feeling a bit self-conscious with all of the attention and pampering I was receiving from Cleary and the Griekos.

The next morning the Griekos and Cleary leave Raven Hill before 8 o'clock. I know the plumber won't be here until 10 or so. I sit at the kitchen table, open my math book. After a few minutes of reading the same line over and over again, I stand up and walk around the house. After walking out of the kitchen, I turn right and stand in the sunroom that overlooks the bay. At the far end of the room is the door to the garage. I decide to turn left and walk into the large living room with its small brick fireplace at one end. On one side of the fireplace is a door that leads to a half bath and on the other side is a door that leads to what Cleary's father used as an office and Cleary now uses to store all of her sewing and handicraft supplies and items.

Suddenly I think of one room I want to look through. I try not to think of myself as snooping around someone else's home, but the desire overpowers me and in a flash I am racing up the stairs and down the hall. I stop before the door to the attic and slowly turn the knob. After opening the door I look into the gloom and see a string hanging down from a bare bulb and pull the string. I climb the narrow steps into the attic. Some light trickles in through the narrow windows and I find another string to pull on and the bare bulb illuminates most of the room. I'm not sure what I am expecting from the attic of Raven Hill, but what I find is a tidy space full of boxes that are neatly stacked on various shelving units. They are all neatly labeled on the outside. Among the boxes are steamer trunks and suitcases covered with stickers with words from several different languages. There are boxes of Christmas ornaments that look freshly packed away. Still other boxes hold summer clothes, family pictures, and several boxes labeled with the words "Calloway Furniture Company" are off a shelf and it is obvious Cleary has been looking through them looking for material for the person in Grand Rapids. One box catches my eye. On the outside "Emily" is written. I take it off the shelf and gently put it down on the floor. I take off the lid and look inside. It seems to be filled with handicraft items, such as needlepoint and embroidery samplers that are partly finished. A few miss- matched hair barrettes and a half-empty bottle of pink nail polish are also included. At the bottom of the box I catch a glimpse of a picture and reach down and pick it up. It is a school picture of a blonde girl, who I instantly recognize as Fair Emily. I turn it over and written in a childish scrawl is "Emily, 6th grade."

What are Emily's belongings doing in Cleary's attic? Did Cleary find them somewhere? Why wouldn't she return them? I put the items back in the box and place the box back on the shelf. I am feeling quite guilty by then and am about to leave when I glance up above one of the attic windows and see a shelf with a small wooden box set upon it. I reach up into the gloom and pull it off the shelf. It isn't heavy, but I can tell there are several items shifting around inside. I set it down on the floor but find that it is locked. Just then I hear the doorbell and realize the plumber has arrived. I quickly return the box to its solitary shelf and hurry down the stairs, pulling on the strings to shut off the lights on my way.

I arrive at the door out of breath and fling open the door. I find Mr. Westerly, the plumber, just about ready to give up finding anyone at home. "I'm sorry, I was upstairs and it's a long run," I try to explain.

"Why Kevin Thorpe, I heard you were staying out here. I guess you can believe some of the gossip you hear."

I confirm to him why I had come to stay at Raven Hill and show him to the kitchen where the nonfunctioning dishwasher is located. I stay in the kitchen and chat while he works and an hour later, when he is finished, show him back out the door, locking it behind him. It is too early for lunch, so I settle back down at the table and open my math book again. However, my mind keeps returning to the attic and the box marked "Emily" and the locked box above the window. I struggle to keep my mind focused on the task at hand. Finally I complete the last of my homework problems and practice my spelling words for the coming week. It is mid-afternoon before I close my spelling book, thinking of what other homework I need to complete before Monday. Well, there is a chapter in my social studies book I should re-read before the test on Wednesday. I climb the stairs to my room and exchange my math book for the social studies book and am about to go back down the stairs when I turn around and head for the attic door. I just put my hand on the doorknob when I hear a door open downstairs. I quickly let go of the doorknob and walk to the head of the stairs. It is Cleary.

"Hi, Kev. Did you have a nice day? Did the plumber show up?"

I make my way down the stairs and assure her that the day went fine and yes, the plumber did show up and apparently fixed the problem.

"I felt so bad leaving you here all by yourself. What kind of host am I anyway?"

"I had a nice day. I got a lot of my homework done." Well, I had. Sort of. "How was your meeting with the guy in Grand Rapids?"

"It went really well. Now that I know what he is looking for, I am going to go through the records and souvenirs that my dad kept again. He wants to borrow some pieces of furniture too. I told him it would be easier to just come up and look through the house when he gets a chance." Her face is glowing and she has a smile on her face. I realize she hasn't looked this happy since I came to Raven Hill. "Yep, it will be great seeing the Calloway Furniture Company name again."

"What happened to the Calloway Furniture Company?"

Her smile fades somewhat. "It closed its doors shortly before my father died in 1960."

"You didn't want to run the company?"

"Yes…no. I really had no idea how to run a company. I was only 25 and my brother only 20. My mother wasn't interested and in reality the heyday of furniture making in Grand Rapids was long over. I'm surprised we were able to stay in business and be profitable for as long as we did."

"Was furniture making a big business in Grand Rapids?"

"Oh my, yes! It started in the middle of the 1800's and several small workshops opened up. Michigan was famous for its lumbering industry. Of course the furniture companies used the hardwood located in the southern half of the state rather than the softer pinewood lumbered in the northern half of the state. Toward the late 1800's larger workshops mass-produced furniture. In fact, Grand Rapids was so famous for furniture that they exhibited their pieces at the World's Exposition in New Orleans in 1884 and at the Chicago World's Fair in 1893. My great-grandmother wrote in her diary about attending both. Calloway Furniture was exhibited at both events, of course!"

"How many companies made furniture?"

"Hmmm…all together I would guess a couple of hundred. Not all at the same time, some came and went. But over the years there were probably a few hundred."

"People would come to Grand Rapids to buy furniture?"

"Yes, some would come and look through the showrooms and take the furniture with them or special order some items. Generally buyers from other stores throughout the United States would come and look over what several companies had to offer and place orders for their shops. The pieces would then be shipped either by ship or train in the early days, and later by truck."

We talk about the furniture business for the next hour. Cleary's face is quite animated as she shares her knowledge of the topic, which is considerable. It is well past nightfall before she stops herself. "Goodness, I've prattled on forever. I'm going to go back to the attic and look through some more boxes. Go ahead and finish any home-work you may have. Since it's Saturday night you can stay up as late as you want. Just remember we have church tomorrow."

I nod in reply, feeling even guiltier about my earlier snooping and slightly afraid that she might discover I have been in the attic. That fear turns out to be groundless as she goes upstairs and when she appears several hours later, nothing is mentioned.

Early the next morning I am shaken awake by Cleary. "Get up Kev. Just enough time for breakfast before we must leave for church."

The four of us eat a hurried breakfast of scrambled eggs and toast before dressing and climbing into the station wagon that Mr. Griekos is driving.

"Oh no! I forgot my purse!" exclaims Cleary before he has a chance to put the car into reverse. She walks quickly back into the house.

Mr. Griekos turns back to me in the back seat. "It's good to have Cleary joining Rose and I for church. I guess we have you to thank."

Now that I think about it, I don't remember seeing Cleary in church before. I just figured she sat far away from our usual seats or went to another church altogether.

"Why?"

"Well now she has someone to look after. She hasn't had that since Emily." At that Rose shoots her husband a look.

"Since Emily? Emily Vanneste? Why did she look after Emily?"

Mr. Griekos looks decidedly uncomfortable. He gives his wife a look that seems to say that the cat is out of the bag already. "Emily's mother's parents were quite elderly and not in good health. She and Frank went to Chicago to straighten out their financial affairs and move them here to Traverse City. It took a few weeks and they decided Cleary would enjoy looking after her. But please Kevin; do not repeat this to anyone. Especially to Old Lady Vanneste. She would be so angry she would just explode."

Just then Cleary opens the back door and slides into the seat next to me. We all jump with surprise.

"What's the matter, didn't think I was coming back?"

"We were just busy chatting," Mr. Griekos answers smoothly as he backs the car away from the house and heads off to town. I sit back into my seat and look out the window. The statement about Lydia Vanneste whirls through my head. What did he mean she would explode? Didn't his own father mention something about a relative of hers dying in an explosion? Did Mrs. Vanneste cause the explosion?

Mr. Griekos let us out at the front door and I have just entered the sanctuary when I am enveloped into the arms of a young woman wearing way too much perfume.

"Oh Kev! I have missed you so much!"

I surprise myself by telling Debbie I have missed her too. I have, but there are some things a little brother should not say too often. Even Missy gives me a big hug. Like my sister she also seems to go heavy on the perfume.

I sit next to Debbie, who is sitting with Missy's family. The Griekos and Cleary are sitting behind us. We talk quietly during most of the service about the last week. Debbie has had a call from our mother who had nothing new to report about our cousins and aunt and uncle. It didn't look like she would be coming home soon. Debbie said Mom planned to call me that night.

After services we gather in the church anteroom and are making our good-byes when Lydia Vanneste is exiting the sanctuary on the arm of her son Frank. She gives us all a long, hard look before her eyes lock on Cleary.

"I wondered why you were showing your face in church. I found out you were watching the Thorpe boy. I would think his father could find someone better suited."

I want to say something, but I can only stand there with my mouth agape. Everyone else seems to be in shock as well, as no one said a word in the seconds that followed her statement and Frank Vanneste throwing Cleary an apologetic look and walking his mother out the door.

Missy's mother saves the day when she quickly speaks up. "After church next week why don't all of you come to our home and have dinner? The kids could have longer to talk."

Cleary and the Griekos agree and a few minutes later we separate and with Cleary walking several yards ahead of the Griekos and I, make our way back to the station wagon.

"Oh that Lydia! What I would like to do with her!" Mr. Griekos mutters under his breath.

Rose sighs, "Well, she has had a rough life too. But really!"

I don't say a word. I am rather frightened by the old woman. The thoughts about Mrs. Vanneste and some explosion keep popping up in my head.

It is later that afternoon as I sit in the living room watching a basketball game on TV that I hear Mr. Griekos in the kitchen talking to Cleary.

"Cleary, if you'd rather, Rose and I can take Kevin to church next week and we can swing by here afterwards and pick you up before going over to the Flemings for dinner."

"No. I'm going," she replies in a voice that makes sure that there is to be no further discussion on the matter.

CHAPTER 13

✿

The following day at school my teacher welcomes us back from the weekend with the reminder that parent-teacher conferences are scheduled for that week. Glances are exchanged amongst the students who have the most to worry about from their teachers talking to their parents. The next announcement is the assignment of our spring project. Every year the fifth and sixth graders are expected to complete a project either individually or in pairs. The topic changes from year to year. Last year they had to put on a science fair. This year we are assigned the task of putting on a job fair. We are to pick an occupation and know its history, salary, outlook, and where the person with that job would work. We are given one week to decide if we are to complete it alone or in pairs and what occupation we want to highlight.

Most of the other kids scramble to team up with someone else. I am suddenly aware that none of my friends are running to my side to ask me to work with them. I sit stupidly in my seat and watch everyone else chattering away and already arguing about what occupation they want to work on. I stay seated there with my eyes downcast until the teacher calls for quiet and everyone to regain their seats so she can begin the days lessons.

At lunch I finally get up the nerve to confront Ted and Tony about the snub. After several minutes of hemming and hawing, Ted finally admits, "Geez Kev, you're living at Raven Hill with that weird woman."

"She is not weird!"

"OK, OK. She has always been nice to me too. But Kev, everyone knows about yesterday at your church. I know and I don't even go to your church."

"So what about it?"

"Well, frankly, none of us want that old woman angry at us because it might hurt my social standing in the community."

"You're social standing? Ted you have no social standing in this town!"

"Actually I'm just repeating what my mom was saying."

"Your mom? Why was she talking about it?"

"This is a small town Kev. She's afraid that with your parents leaving you with Miss Calloway that your family will never be invited to another function at Oak Lawn."

"What does any of this have to do with working with me on a project?"

"We're afraid that if we are seen at Raven Hill we and our families will be on the outs with the old lady too. Honestly Kev, it would kill my mom not to go to that Christmas party."

I can't believe it. Here we are, ten year olds and worried about not being invited to a Christmas party. "That is the most stupid thing I have ever heard."

"Did you know that every year the old lady hosts a party after the spring musical? Isn't your sister in 'South Pacific' this year?"

"Yes, she is in it. She was in 'Guys and Dolls' last year and we all went to Oak Lawn for a party after the last performance."

"Well, I wouldn't count on being invited this year."

That did it. I pick up my tray off the table and throw it away in the trash and walk back to the classroom where I put on my coat and hat and go outside for the remaining minutes of our lunch hour.

Later that evening as I sit up in bed reading a book assigned in school, a knock comes at the door. It is Cleary. "Is everything OK Kevin? You were so quiet at dinner and you didn't want to play cards with Mr. Griekos like you usually do."

"Oh I'm fine. I just got a lot of homework and I'm thinking about my project in school."

"What project is that?"

"We have to choose a job and set up a booth and answer people's questions about it."

"You mean an occupation? What have you selected?"

"I haven't decided yet."

"Well, what would you like to do when you grow up?"

"I was thinking of being a baseball player, or a cowboy or maybe an Indian."

At the mention of the last one Cleary can't quite hide a small smile. "Perhaps you could do my occupation."

I stare at her blankly. "You don't have a job."

She looks rather taken aback. "True, I haven't worked in a long time. But I used to be a nurse."

"Really? I didn't know."

"Well, how could you?" She suddenly looks rather upset, but struggling to stay cheerful she smiles, "I guess I'll leave you to your reading and I'm sure you'll think of something for your project." With that she turns and walks out of the room, quietly closing the door behind her.

Yawning, I shut my book and put it on the nightstand and turn off the light. I lay there for a while in the silence before I drift off. Sometime later I hear the faint sounds of a door shutting downstairs. Curious, I climb out of bed and part the curtains to see if I can see anything. The moon and the stars cast a soft light over the deep snow on the lawn. I catch sight of a dark figure making it's way toward the stand of trees that stand between the lawn of Raven Hill and the cemetery. Once the figure reaches the trees, a light goes on and it continues into the woods until it disappears. I lay back down and wonder about Cleary going to the cemetery at this late of an hour. Maybe the kids at school are right, maybe she is weird. But try as I might, I can't bring myself to dislike her, even if my whole family becomes social outcasts of Traverse City.

The next day after dinner, Cleary excuses herself and drives to my school by herself. It is parent-teacher conferences and she is acting as my parent. I figure my teachers will only say nice things about me to my temporary parent, but you never know. As I try to relax in front of the TV, I spy Cleary's sewing basket on the end table. Something is sticking out and the curiosity overwhelms me. I open the padded lid and lift out the large piece of yellow material. It is a small baby quilt. The top has been cross-stitched and depicts Noah and his ark. Cleary was still working on closing the seams. I look into the basket again and find a few pairs of crocheted baby booties and a few tiny outfits. I gently put the items back and place the basket back on the end table. Like the attic I feel guilty, but can't help snooping.

A few minutes later, I hear the door open to the kitchen and I go to find Cleary taking her boots off and placing them next to the door.

"How did it go?"

She looks up, surprised to see me standing there. "Why, your teachers had nothing but nice things to say about you. You must take after your mother," she teases. "It was fun, playing mom, at least for one night."

We go into the living room where she continues to talk about her evening with my teachers. She sits down on the couch and reaches for the sewing basket. She takes out the quilt and holds it up. "What do you think?"

"Is it for Emily?"

"Yes, you know her baby is due in a few more months."

"What will…ah…Mrs…"

"What will Mrs. Vanneste say?"

I nod.

"I don't care," she snaps. "The gift is for Emily and her baby."

For some reason I think back to what Ted had said at school the previous day. I wonder what Mom will say when they aren't invited to the Christmas party next year.

I sit beside her and admire her handiwork. Well, I won't miss that party, at least not that much.

CHAPTER 14

After a few weeks Raven Hill begins to feel like home. Sure, I miss my parents and sisters, but I usually talk to them by phone at least once a week and I usually spend Sunday with Debbie either at the Fleming's home or Debbie and the Flemings would visit Raven Hill for Sunday dinner. Luckily we managed to avoid another run-in with Lydia Vanneste. The Griekos and Frank Vanneste seem to have worked out a method of arriving and departing from church at different times.

Life falls into a comfortable routine and before I know it, it is the end of February. The last Saturday of that month turns out to be sunny and mild. After breakfast is finished and I help Rose wash and dry the dishes, Cleary comes into the kitchen and announces, "I am so tired of staying inside and it's supposed to be nearly 50 degrees today, so let's all go outside and get some work done. Does that sound OK to everyone?"

Rose shrugs, "I guess I could use some fresh air myself. I'm sure Sal has gone back to our apartment, but I can get him when I'm done here. I've noticed the garage is a mess, but it's been too cold for him to stay out there and tidy up. This might be a good time to do that."

Cleary nods in agreement. "There are piles of leaves in the garden area, and if I can start on raking those out of there today it would save time in the spring. You can help me Kev."

I nod. I am rather tired of working on my career project anyway.

An hour later I am raking the dead leaves of last fall that have congregated around the fountain in the garden. Cleary stops her raking that she has been doing around a trellis and comes to stand next to me. "I guess I had better check the statue. Last year it looked like it might be developing a crack and this cold weather we have had wouldn't help."

She climbs into the fountain's basin and begins to untie the rope that holds the burlap snuggly around the statue. She then unravels the burlap and exposes the figure of the boy and girl standing under the umbrella that I had admired the summer before at Emily's wedding reception. Without the water running over the figures, I could better see the details of the little boy and girl.

Cleary notices me staring intently at the faces of the statues. "Does the face of the girl look familiar?"

I am startled by her voice "Yes…it looks…like *you*."

She laughs. "Well, it *is* me! My father commissioned it on one of our travels to Italy. The artist spent a whole day sketching my brother and I. Then he took several pictures of us holding an umbrella over our heads, even though it was 90 degrees and sunny." She chuckles at the memory.

I look at the faces again. The girl does indeed look like the young face I had seen in my father's photograph. My attention turns to the young boy, whose face is tilted up toward the girl's, with an almost hero-worshipping expression.

"Then that is your brother," I state rather than ask.

She smiles softly, gently stroking the metal face with her finger. "Yes, its Ezra. It looks so much like him."

"My dad says he died in Vietnam."

She nods in reply.

"Is he buried in the cemetery over there?" I'm not sure why I ask the question as I already know he is buried in Grand Rapids.

She looks at me oddly and replies, "No, he is buried in Grand Rapids. My family has a vault there."

"Are you going to be buried in Grand Rapids too?"

"No...ye..." She hesitates and looks undecided.

"I'm sorry, my parents would call that a 'morbid' question."

She looks at me and laughs. "I would agree. It's a beautiful day, let's talk about something more cheerful." She turns back to the statue and examines it closely, looking for any cracks and chips. Finding it in good condition, she wraps the burlap around the figures and reties the rope.

Trying to change the topic to a happier one I ask, "Did you do a lot of traveling? Growing up I mean."

I help her out of the basin and hand her back her rake.

"Oh yes! I missed plenty of school. Oh I had a tutor all right, but my father liked to travel three or four months out of the year. He would say it was to inspect various furniture factories, but I think he just enjoyed visiting other places. We usually spent the summers here because the weather was nice. It's a wonder I made it through school," she finished with a laugh.

"Where did you go?"

"Oh, where *didn't* we go? Most of the travels were in Europe or Great Britain. We did go as far as Japan and Australia."

"Really?" I can't imagine going to such exotic places. "Where was the last place you went to?"

A shadow briefly crossed her face. "Vietnam."

"Oh. You went there after your brother died?"

She shook her head. "I was there when he died."

"You were in the army?" I asked incredulously.

The shadow lifted slightly. "I was a nurse Kev. I was stationed in Vietnam."

"Oh. You went to be with your brother?"

"Yes...no...Oh there you are!"

I turn to find Mr. Griekos walking toward us with the day's mail in his hands. She drops the rake and it falls to the ground with a loud "clunk". She takes the mail from him and continues back to the house and goes inside. Mr. Griekos walks up to me. "How is it going, Kev? Getting a lot done?" And then he looks at my sad expression and adds, "Is something wrong?"

I shrug. "I was asking her about her brother and her being a nurse in Vietnam. I guess she doesn't like to talk about it, does she?"

He smiles at me and picks up the rake Cleary had dropped and goes to work at the leaves still piled about. "Oh, she likes to talk about her brother. It's been enough time since then. But no, she doesn't like to talk about Vietnam."

"I guess it must have been…bad." Actually I have no idea what it must have been like. I was too young to remember anything about the Vietnam War. I had heard people mention it. My experience with any war was limited to the movies on T.V. I guess cleaning up all that gore and blood would be a bad experience for anyone, especially someone as sensitive as Cleary seemed to be.

Mr. Griekos looks like he would have said more but he purses his lips together and doesn't reply.

Later that afternoon, after the yard work is completed, Cleary asks if I want to see some pictures of her travels around the world. I answer in the affirmative and she asks that I follow her upstairs. We pass the door to my room and down the hall, where she stops in front of the door to the attic. She opens it and I follow her up the narrow steps. She turns, pulls on the strings hanging from the ceiling and the bare bulbs illuminate the room. She crosses the room and stands in front of the shelves holding various boxes. Some of them are ones I had already peeked into when I had sneaked up to the attic several weeks before. She pulls a large box off a shelf and places it on the floor. She opens the top and I can see several photo albums inside. She pulls one out and we take our seats on the floor and she begins to show me the yellowed pictures inside.

It is two hours later that, sensing I am tired, she closes the album we are looking through. "I guess that's enough for now. It must be time for dinner, let's go see what Rose has fixed for us."

"That was great, Cleary. Were those all the photographs?"

She laughed. "Oh no, that was just Italy, France and Germany. We still have Great Britain, Japan, and well, at least a dozen more. Like I said, my father liked to travel. I guess we all did."

"How come you don't travel now?"

"I guess...I guess...I've seen enough." She answers softly, not meeting my gaze but looking intently at the small wooden box that is placed by itself on a shelf over the attic window. The conversation obviously over, she pulls on the strings hanging from the ceiling, leaving us in the gloom of the attic. She starts down the stairs and before following her I look intently at the box. I know it is locked. For some reason I can't explain, I suddenly want to open that box. Where could the key be? With one last look I go down the stairs and close the door behind me. Before going to the kitchen I make a stop at my bathroom and while washing my hands I hear someone pass by the closed door.

I make my way to the kitchen and find Rose and Mr. Griekos setting the table and preparing dinner.

"It will just be us for dinner Kev, Cleary said she needed to lay down for awhile."

"Did I say something wrong?"

Rose simply pats my shoulder and points to the chair at the table I am to sit in. "I wouldn't worry, Kev. She gets like this occasionally. She will be back to her old self tomorrow."

Even with her kind words I feel bad. I wouldn't hurt Cleary for the world. Was it talking about her brother or was it about the travels as a child with her family that had upset her? Perhaps if I knew I could make it all better, I reasoned with my ten-year-old brain. My mind keeps going back to that mysterious box. Somehow I have the feeling that the answer is to be found in it.

"Now don't worry, Kev," Mr. Griekos broke into my thoughts. "You'll see, things will be fine tomorrow."

Indeed, the next day Cleary acted as if nothing had happened.

Later that same week, Cleary picks me up from school with the news that she has insisted that the Griekos take a much-needed day off from work. "I was thinking that we could try out that new pizzeria downtown for dinner. Would you like that?"

I hesitate. Except for trips to the library, church services, and her picking me up and dropping me off at school, Cleary and I haven't been seen in public together. But I look at her smiling face and find I can't hurt her feelings by saying no, so I answer that I would love to try the restaurant and pizza was my favorite food, which is true.

We go to Raven Hill and I change my clothes and wash up and start my homework before Cleary calls from the bottom of the stairs and says it's time to go. We find a parking spot on the street and walk to the main entrance of the restaurant that still has the "Grand Opening" banner hanging from the roof. A young man comes to greet us and to seat us in a booth in front that overlooks the main street. Cleary settles in and begins to chat excitedly about the furniture show in Grand Rapids that summer. I try to listen but I am distracted by the sight of people doing double takes as they walk by on the street or pass by in the restaurant on their way to their own tables. Cleary doesn't seem to notice. We look at the extensive menu and together decide on a deep-dish pepperoni and green olives pizza and give our order to the waitress who also seems surprised at the sight of Cleary in her restaurant. Cleary has just started talking about the summer furniture show when an excited squeal fills the air and a woman bustles over from a nearby table. Cleary has a surprised look that becomes a smile when she stands up to give the woman a warm hug.

"Mary! So nice to see again! Are you visiting from Vermont?"

"Yes, yes. My husband Marty and the kids are sitting over there." She points to a table that an elderly couple, a man and two college-aged children were sitting. "The kids are on spring break from college so we all decided to come back to Traverse City and visit with my folks for the week."

Cleary turns back to me. "Mary, this is Kevin Thorpe. You remember Thomas of course. Well, this is his youngest and he is staying with me until his parents come home. They have had to go out of town on personal business."

Mary nods. "My folks have told me all the local news."

I hold my breath, but Cleary doesn't bat an eye at the comment.

Cleary continues, "Kev, this is Mary Jones, or should I say Mary Stein. She was one our gang when your father and I were growing up."

I nod, suddenly remember my father mentioning a Mary Jones who had moved to Vermont. "Nice to meet you Mrs. Stein."

"Nice to meet Tommy's little boy. He was such a nice kid when we were growing up."

I merely nod in reply. I can't really imagine my father being a kid and hanging out with girls, no matter how nice they seem.

Mary turns back to her family and points out, "The blonde girl who looks most like me is Robin and the dark haired one is Mariette. I named her after our friend."

Cleary nodded. "Poor Mariette. She was such a sweet girl."

"And of course I heard what had happened to Robert. I guess those two were never meant to be. I hope Robbie had some happiness before he died."

"I know he did…" is all that Cleary is able to get out before our pizza arrives and Mary excuses herself to let us eat in peace before their food arrives.

When we finish eating, Mary comes back over to our table and chats for a few minutes before she leaves with her family. "It was good to see you again, Cleary, I hope we meet again."

I am finishing my soft drink when an older man approaches with our bill. "Why hello Cleary! I hope your remember me…"

"Of course I do Mr. Goodspeed! I didn't realize this was your restaurant."

"Actually it's my nephew's, but I'm here helping him out for the first weeks while they work out the bugs. *Not* that we have bugs…" he teases.

They chat for a few minutes before he excuses himself. "Well, back to the kitchen. I hope to see more of you in the future Cleary, and not just in the restaurant."

A few minutes later we walk down the sidewalk and Cleary clasps my hand in hers. "You know, tonight was fun. I had forgotten what it was like to get out of the house for a while and socialize with others."

I smile up at her and notice that she seems to have acquired a bounce in her step.

CHAPTER 15

❀

My tie is cutting into my neck and I can barely breath as I struggled to loosen the knot that keeps jabbing me in the Adams apple. I stand alone in front of the display I have worked so hard to put together. I even printed off a whole stack of handouts explaining the education and exciting career of a Certified Public Accountant.

All the children from the public and private schools and the general public are invited. We are expected to spend the entire day extolling the virtues of our chosen topic. Since I worked by myself, I am afraid I won't get a break at all, but Cleary comes to the rescue and promises all three of them will come and give me a break and most importantly, keep me company.

I look over to see my friends, Ted and Tony; they have a large crowd standing about their display. They had signed up early and got one of the more popular occupations, that of police officer. They had even talked one of the local officers to come in and talk to the visitors for an hour or so. It is obvious that they will be receiving one of the highest grades in the class. I am hoping for a **C**.

The Griekos stop by in the morning, giving me a few minutes to relax and wander about the gymnasium and get a better look at my competition. Most, like me, have posters and handouts. A few have brought in TVs and VCRs and are playing tapes that demonstrate some aspect of their topic. I stop and stare at the tape brought in by the pair of students who had landed the occupation of physician. They are running a tape of some man's knee operation. I think it is a little gory, but judging from the number of others gathered around, it is a huge hit. Somewhat disheartened I make my way back to my booth and find the Griekos sitting in front of my display. Alone.

The afternoon starts off the same way until Cleary arrives. She is wearing a wide smile and breezes past the other displays on her way to my table. I am grateful that she didn't seem to notice the other people glancing her way and murmuring about her behind her back.

"Hi Kev! How is it going? Rose said the career day expo was a bit hit."

"Well, we have had a lot of people coming through. Oh yea, you should have been here when Ted's brother Brad was handcuffed by the visiting policeman! It was so funny! The officer pretended that he had forgotten the key and you should have seen the look on Brad's face!"

Cleary joins me in my laughter. "I'm sorry I missed that. Let's hope that's the last time he is in handcuffs."

Knowing Brad as well as I do, I hope so too.

We keep each other company while I explain the wonderful world of a CPA to the few people that venture close enough for me to snag them into conversation. Even then most of the people seem to only pretend to listen to me while their eyes seem to be staring in Cleary's direction.

Finally 3 o'clock comes and it is time to clean up. While I am gathering up my belongings, Cleary suddenly says, "Look behind you, Kev."

I glance up and I catch the sight of my parents winding their way through the gymnasium towards me. With a cry of joy I drop what I am holding in my hands and run towards them and throw myself into both of their arms.

We all start to talk at once until my father holds up his hand. "OK, OK, one at a time. You first Kevin."

I am still in shock but manage to sputter, "What are you doing here?"

"Well, my work is slowing down and everyone is out of the hospital, so we thought we would surprise you. And, as if you couldn't forget, tomorrow is your sister's birthday."

"I didn't forget," seeing the look on my father's face. "I already got her a card and a small gift. We were all invited…I mean Cleary, the Griekos, and I were invited to the Flemings for dinner tomorrow night."

"We will call the Flemings tonight and see what we want to do to celebrate Debbie's birthday. Can we help you pack up your display?"

Cleary speaks up, "It's nearly picked up. Why don't you go on home and I will take it back to my house."

"Thanks so much Cleary," both of my parents say as they each take one of my hands and we walk out of the school together for the first time as a family in two months.

"Kevin, I'm so proud you picked the occupation of Certified Public Accountant for your project. Was it because of me being a CPA?"

"No. It was the only topic left and Mrs. Cutler said I couldn't select the job of cowboy. I bet people would have found that interesting," I say with an envious sigh thinking how popular some of the other exhibits had been.

My mom's shoulders shake and I ask what is wrong. She wipes away the tears around her eyes and tries to wipe the smile off her lips when she replies, "It's just nice to be home again." My father just shakes his head.

We then drive to the high school and walk down the long silent corridors to the auditorium. We let ourselves in a side door and find seats in the house. On the stage several teenagers stand around listening to what the lone adult in front of them is telling them "…when she starts singing, I need to see the other nurses come towards the audience…but this time try not to knock Nelly into the orchestra pit, OK?"

Just then one of the "nurses" lets out a shriek and runs down the stage steps toward us. It is Debbie wearing an odd ensemble, for March anyway, consisting of a Hawaiian shirt, short shorts, and a straw hat.

She squeals with delight as she hugs our parents once and then again. After a few words of greeting she rejoins her cast mates on the stage. We spend the next hour watching the students run through several song and dance numbers and I have to admit that even I am impressed. As Debbie sits in the back seat on the way home she turns to me. "So, Kev, you *are* coming to see me in the play next weekend aren't you?"

"Well, I was dragged to 'Guys and Dolls' last year and 'Seven Brides for Seven Brothers' the year before that and 'The Sound of Music' when you were in junior high school. So, yea, I guess I'll see this one." I breathe a heavy sigh like it is going to be pure torture for me.

"I take that as a yes?"

I nod. "I'm sure the Griekos and Cleary would love to see it."

"Ahhhh…I don't know about Cleary," my father speaks up from the driver's seat.

"Why not? She has told me all about plays and operas she has seen all around the world. Showed me some play bills she had kept."

Silence greets me, as my father seems to be struggling for something to say. But I speak up before he has found the words. "It's because she was a nurse in Vietnam and her brother died there, isn't it?"

"….And Robert."

"And Robert," I add, not quite sure why he added Mrs. Vanneste's son. I turn back to Debbie. "I'll be there. I wouldn't miss you making a fool of yourself in public."

She grabs me with one arm around my neck and rubs my head, hard, with her knuckles. "I can't tell you how much I've missed doing that."

"OK, you two," our mother warns from the front seat. She sighs, "I can't wait to come back to this."

"When are you coming back for good?"

"Either next weekend or the week after that. I can't promise I'll be here for your play, Deb. Sorry."

"Me too, Hon," my father adds. "I don't think I'll finish my work until the end of March."

"That's OK guys. We tape the final dress rehearsal and sell copies in the lobby. I'll buy one if you can't make it. Besides, you'd just make me nervous anyway."

"Gee thanks. Here I thought we brought you luck! I will miss the reception at Oak Lawn though. That's always a good time."

"Oh yea, Mrs. Vanneste has always invited the entire cast and their families. I guess that means you can come with me, Kev."

I nod, but I wonder if I will be welcome at Oak Lawn ever again.

We pull into our driveway and we pile out of the car and I enter the house for the first time in weeks. My parents had arrived there earlier and turned up the heat and bought a few groceries for the weekend.

Oddly, I find it strange to be back in my own home. Compared to Raven Hill my home seems small and cramped. I find I can't find anything I want and have to search my own drawers and closet for items I want to take back for my last week or so at Raven Hill. After a while I wander down the hall to my parents room and flop on their bed while they are shuffling through their drawers and closet for items they wish to take back with them.

"Tom, I'm afraid I need some more spending money. Mom and Dad offered to pay me, but well, I 'd feel funny, and I am staying at their house and eating their food."

My father nods. "The store is going to reimburse me my expenses, but not for another few weeks. Let's go ahead and crack open the emergency fund and we'll just pay it back in a month."

My mom nods in agreement and walks over to her dresser and pulls open one of the tiny drawers of her jewelry box and pulls out a key.

"What's that?"

"It's the key to the safe. I guess it's an obvious hiding place. Maybe I should find a new place? Huh?"

My father shrugs, "It's up to you. But really we have a safe because it won't burn in a fire, not because we have anything of much value."

I follow my mother into the walk-in closet and watch as she opens the floor safe. She reaches in and pulls out a bankbook.

"What's that?"

"It's the savings account that we set up for emergencies just like we have now."

I point at the rest of the papers and other items still in the safe. "What's all that?"

"Actually it may be a good idea you know what's in here. Just in case." She takes out various items and explains what they are. "Here are everyone's birth certificates. Here are your vaccination records. My grandmother's wedding ring. The deed to the house and the insurance papers for our cars. A copy of our will that hopefully you won't need for a while. And here is something you might get a kick out of."

She hands me a heavy, folded piece of paper. I unfold it and read out loud what it says: "Joined together in holy matrimony on this day of July 8th 1961 are Thomas Eric Thorpe and Laura Elizabeth McMurry…Hey! That's you!"

My mom laughs and my dad pokes his head around the corner of the closet. "I thought we burned that…"

I return the document back to her and she places everything back into the safe and hands me the key and asks for me to replace it back where she had found it.

As I open the tiny drawer of the jewelry box, a thought crosses my mind. "Is this where women hide things?"

My father shrugs. "I suppose it depends on the size of what they are hiding."

To me it was just the right size.

❦   ❦   ❦

The next evening just the four of us sit around the dinner table. It being Debbie's seventeenth birthday, it is left up to her to decide what she wants to do for her big day. She decides to just have her immediate family, except Kathy who is unable to attend, for dinner. And she decides to just have a home cooked roast rather than go out to a restaurant. While the Flemings had planned to host a dinner that would have included the Griekos and Cleary, everyone understood that she just wanted a small dinner with her parent and brother instead.

We enjoy the meal that my mother cooked as much as if it had come from an expensive restaurant. A small stack of gifts sit at Kathy's place at the table. Debbie opens the gifts after dinner and before Mom lights the candles of the cake she had picked up at the bakery earlier that day. Mom had bought her a new pair of shorts with two matching tops which brought the comment from dad that perhaps she could wear that outfit instead of the skimpy outfit she was wearing for the play.

"What exactly is 'South Pacific' about anyway?"

"It's during World War II in the South Pacific…as you may have guessed from the title. Nelly is the main character and Eleanor Busby plays her. She falls in love with this French guy on the island played by Mark Andrews. Meanwhile everyone sings and dances around on the beach." She laughed. "It's better than I make it sound, trust me!"

"I hope so!" I hand her my gift and she rips off the paper with one motion.

"Oooohhh! Thank you Kev!" She squirts a few drops of the perfume on her wrist and sniffs. "I always wanted some 'Rose Mystic'! Thank you Kev."

I was pleased. Cleary had suggested the gift when we had gone shopping downtown a few weeks ago. I figured she had better taste in perfume than I did, and apparently, she did.

Debbie leans back in her chair and with a smile she states "This has been so great! While I've had a good time with Missy and her family, I miss all of you. I can't wait until we can be a family again."

"What about you Kev?" my father inquires. "How are things at Raven Hill?"

"Cleary and the Griekos have been really great. And wow! The house is so huge! But I can't wait until you can come home either." I don't dare mention that staying with Cleary has made me somewhat of an outcast with my peers and apparently has ruined any chances of a future social life in Traverse City.

CHAPTER 16

❀

My parents drop me off at school that Monday and then continue on in their separate directions. It is hard to say good-bye after being together again for such a short time. I wave until they each drive out of sight before heading into the school building. I walk to my classroom and take my seat next to Ted and Tony.

As I sit down, Steve, a classmate who usually barely acknowledges my existence leans over and whispers, "So Kev, I see your parents are home. Must be happy to be away from that creepy Miss Calloway, huh?"

I can hear Ted and Tony catch their breaths in unison. I look Steve right in the eye and for a reason I still cannot understand state, "Look, she isn't creepy and unlike Old Mrs. Vanneste, she doesn't blow someone up!"

Unfortunately not only did Steve hear me, but everyone around us did too.

"What are you talking about?" Steve demands.

I hesitate. What should I say? I somehow find my voice and blurt out, "My dad told me that after she got dumped by Miss Calloway's father, she went nuts and blew up a relative! Actually, I bet she blew up *a lot* of people! Maybe she'll go nuts again!"

"Whaaaat?"

"It's true. I don't know how, but she blew up a relative of hers! My father said so and he has known the Calloways and the Vannestes all his life!"

A collective gasp goes up around me. And then a loud buzz begins as the news quickly spreads to the people who are not close enough to hear it for themselves.

"Miss Calloway's father dumped Mrs. Vanneste?" someone whispered. I blanche when I realize that was information that I had not meant to release, but it is too late now. Oh, it is too late all right.

Just then our teacher walks into the classroom. Normally she finds us half-asleep or quietly conversing with others. This morning she finds us in an uproar.

"What is going on here?" she demands.

Conversation comes to an immediate end and several make a dive for their assigned seats. We must look mighty guilty, as she continues to stare at us long after we sit down and face forward.

"Does anyone have anything to say?"

No one says a word. After several uncomfortable moments, she begins to write the day's lessons on the board. I sit hunched over a piece a paper, pretending to be absorbed into the task at hand and trying not to notice all the eyes that keep glancing my way.

It is with great relief that it is Rose who picks me up that afternoon after school. The peace and quiet of Raven Hill is most welcome after the day's events for which I am entirely responsible.

At supper that evening I decide to bring up the subject of the play. "Remember when I told you Debbie was in a play? Well, it's this weekend. Do all of you want to go?"

Rose brightened. "Oh yes, the spring musical! Sal and I have gone every year. Of course we'd love to go, especially since we know one of the stars."

"She is just one of the singing nurses."

"Why, I'd love to go too," added Cleary.

"It's 'South Pacific,'" Rose said quietly to Cleary.

"I know."

"It's set during World War II."

"I know." With that she turns back to me. "So, when are the performances?"

"Thursday night is a dress rehearsal that people can go watch. Most people with screaming babies go to that one. Debbie says if you can say your lines with screaming babies in the audience, you can say your lines in front of *any* audience."

Cleary smiles. "I think we can skip that performance."

"The real performances are Friday and Saturday night at 7:30 p.m. and Sunday at one o'clock. After that performance everyone involved with the play goes to Oak Lawn for a party." I hesitate before adding, "My sister wants me to be her date. I hope you don't mind."

Cleary shrugs her shoulders. "I don't mind at all. We can go after church Sunday and I'll ask the Flemings to bring you back here after the party. How does that sound?"

"Great." As I pick up my fork to start eating I glance toward Rose who seems to have a concerned look on her face. To myself I am wondering if I will be welcome at Oak Lawn if Old Mrs. Vanneste ever finds out what I blurted out in school that morning. Well if she does, it probably won't be until after the party is over. So I reason to myself that I had better enjoy this soiree, as it will most likely be my last at Oak Lawn.

This week at school seems to drag as I am continuously asked about my outburst that Monday. I don't have anything else to add, but that doesn't stop the rumor from taking on a life of its own. By Friday the story is that Lydia Vanneste, matriarch of Traverse City, has been involved in a multi-state crime spree involving bank robbing and bombing government buildings. By the time I walk out of school at the end of that week I am happy for two things; one, they haven't traced the rumor back to me and two, no one calls Cleary "creepy"; in fact, no one is even talking about Cleary.

The next day, Saturday, Cleary drives to Grand Rapids to meet with the man who is putting together the furniture exhibit and the Griekos decide to run errands in town. They ask if I wish to come with them, but I beg off, telling them I have too much homework and I won't have a chance to do it the next day because of the party. Actually, I decided to stay home because of something I had seen on Cleary's dresser. Earlier in the week I had asked Cleary for her sewing kit as I had popped a button off my shirt. She had insisted on sewing it on herself and I followed her to her bedroom where she had been working on baby clothes for Emily. As she deftly threaded a needle and quickly sewed my button back on my shirt, I couldn't help but notice on her dresser sat a large jewelry case.

After I wave good-bye to the Griekos and Cleary I sit at the desk in my bedroom, trying to concentrate on my homework. No matter how hard I try, I keep glancing up and looking out the window. I finally stand up and walk over to the window and stare out over the great expanse of white. It is mid-March and the winds are bringing warmer air, but deep snow still covers the lawn. My attention is drawn to the path leading from the house across the lawn and into the woods toward the cemetery. I decide to seize the opportunity of being alone during the day and go downstairs and put on my boots and coat and leave the house. I make my way down the well-trodden path. The wind, while warmer than it has been the last few months, is still biting. I pull my hood over my head and stuff my bare hands into the deep pockets and brace myself against the wind. Relief is finally found when I enter the woods and I relax in the relative warmth of the protected path. But the protection doesn't last long, as it is only a short distance to the cemetery.

The cemetery is deserted, in fact it hasn't been plowed out since the last snow a week or so prior. I follow the path that leads to a cement bench that has been cleared off, in fact, a snow shovel is leaning against a nearby tree. I take a seat on the bench and look around. What did Cleary find so fascinating about this place? True, it is sort of beautiful, in an eerie sort of way, with the snow perched upon the headstones that are clumped here and there. I sit back and relax, enjoying the peace and quiet. Perhaps that is why Cleary liked visiting here. With a start I realize that the headstone directly in front of me has been carefully brushed off. I stand up and walk up and stand in front of it as I read what it says:

Robert Benjamin Vanneste
1940–1963
Beloved son

I look around and find other Vanneste graves, but, oddly, Robert's grave is by itself at the foot of Donald Vanneste, his father. A headstone next to Donald's grave reads:

Lydia Augusta Standish Vanneste
1905–

Leave it to Old Mrs. Vanneste to be prepared. On the other side of her stone is a large, open space, as if someone is supposed to be buried there but isn't, at least not yet.

So Cleary was visiting an old friend? I look over the bay from where I stand. It is still covered with ice, but I know the boats will soon be crowding the water. Wasn't it here, near the cemetery that the boat that his father and the others had been riding in had been struck by another boat? And Robert would have drowned if not for Cleary's quick action? Why did I suddenly think of that? As I stand there lost in my own thoughts, I suddenly realize that the sky has turned gray and snow is beginning to swirl about me. I pull my hood back up over my head and make for the house as fast I can.

I shake off my coat and stomp my boots and after taking them off, leave them beside the kitchen door. I step inside the warm house and shut the door firmly behind me. Leaving my coat on a peg in the kitchen I head up the stairs to the second floor. I meant to go back into my room and continue my studies but my curiosity is piqued and I find myself continuing on to Cleary's bedroom. I hesitate in the doorway, but unable to control myself, I keep walking towards the triple dresser that has the jewelry case set on its top. Slowly and carefully I slide the drawers of the case open and look over their contents. Nothing but jewelry. Finally I come to the bottom drawer and open it. There, beneath an old pocket watch is a small key. I gently push the watch aside and lift out the key and look at it closely. It looks small, old, and darkened with age. It looks like a perfect fit.

Closing the bottom drawer, I turn, and holding the key in front of me, leave the bedroom and make my way to the attic stairs. I have just turned the knob when I hear the kitchen door open and Cleary yelling out, "Is anyone home?"

I am so startled I drop the key. It is a sharp *ping* on the wooden floor and I jump with fright. I bend down and pick up the key and shove it into the pocket of my jeans. I quickly walk back out into the hallway and silently close to the attic door behind me. I tip toe to the top of the stairs and call out, "I'm up here Cleary. I was doing my homework."

Cleary appears at the foot of the stairs and looks up at me. "I had to come back, the roads were a mess and I passed several cars in the ditch. I guess I'll have to make the trip next week sometime. Were you out for a walk?"

"What makes you say that?" I stammer, suddenly in the grips of overwhelming guilt over all that I had done.

"Your boots are by the door. You are allowed to leave the house," she says, giving me a quizzical look.

"Yes, I took a walk. I had to get some fresh air. I was getting tired of my homework."

"That's fine, I remember the feeling."

"Well, I guess I had better get back to work."

"Fine, I'll start lunch and let you know when it's done."

I nod and quickly go back into my room and shut the door behind me. I am actually shaking. I reach into my pocket and look with extreme guilt at the key. That was close, I had almost been caught and here everyone had been so kind to me. I vow to replace the key as soon as I have the chance. I open the top drawer of my nightstand and hide it under some of my school papers. With a sigh I sit down at my desk and open my math book, determined to put the whole matter out of my mind once and for all.

CHAPTER 17

❁

"So, Kev, do you think you'll be home this time next week?"

I swallow hard. While it would be great to see my parents again, I am sure going to miss the delicious meals Rose and Cleary have made for me. "Yea, Dad thinks one or both would be home this week or next." I continue to devour my pancakes on this Sunday morning.

Mr. Griekos looks at me. "We will miss you Kev. You'll have to come back for visits."

I find it easy to answer, "I will."

Just then a loud cracking sound vibrates through the house.

Cleary, startled, drops her fork.

My eyes widen. "What was that?"

Trying to sound calm, but giving Cleary a concerned look, Rose replies, "It's just the ice on the lake. Some years, depending on the weather, when the ice breaks up it sounds like gun fire or thunder."

Cleary picks up the fork and places it next to her half-finished plate and rises to her feet. "I'll go get ready for church." And with that left the room.

"Is she OK?"

"Sure," responds Mr. Griekos as he returns to his breakfast.

I have the feeling that any more questions will not be welcomed. But I can't help but think that it is odd Cleary would be frightened of a sound she must have heard all her life.

After church services the four of us go to a local restaurant for lunch before we attend the play at the local high school. I decide to eat lightly as I assume that plenty of food will be served at the gathering at Oak Lawn. That is, unless I was tossed out by order of Mrs. Lydia Vanneste.

The auditorium is already half full and filling up fast when we find four seats together near the front. The Flemings, Missy's parents, come in soon after us and sit just ahead of us. Mrs. Fleming leans over the back of her seat and whispers "They've had wonderful turnouts for this play. I know Missy and Deb have worked really hard on it. We saw it Friday night and liked it so much we came back again today. Plus we are invited to the party at Oak Lawn because we worked on selling advertising in the program." She stops suddenly, realizing she has mentioned Oak Lawn, the home of Mrs. Vanneste. But Cleary doesn't seem to hear her as she is staring at the photographs of the cast that decorate the front of the program. I glance at the cover of my program but all I can see are pictures of smiling faces of girls in skimpy costumes and boys in sailor uniforms.

The lights dim quickly and come back up for a moment before slowly dimming again. The orchestra begins the overture. I recognize the music as my mother often played Broadway tunes on the stereo at home. When the overture ends, the curtain comes up to reveal a tropical scene and two classmates of mine who have landed the roles of Ngana and Jerome, the two children in the play. The competition for those roles was reminiscent of those competing for a role in Fair Emily's wedding.

I glance periodically at Cleary sitting next to me. She has a happy look on her face and laughs the hardest at the character of "Bloody Mary." She nudges me as the nurses jog across the stage in one of the scenes. "Deb looks really cute in her costume."

I have to admit she does look good in her short shorts and straw hat. In fact all the nurses all look pretty cute.

The sailors on stage have just finished singing "There is Nothin' Like A Dame" when a tall, blonde young man in a uniform walks out onto the stage. I recognize him right away as Chris Webster, a senior who is the object of much female admiration, including my sister. I wonder if he finds her cute in her skimpy costume. While I am pondering that thought I feel Cleary stiffen beside me. I turn her way and see that her smile is gone and she appears to be biting her lip. I feel that something is wrong, but not knowing what, I whisper, "It's Chris Webster. He is playing the part of Joe Cable."

"Yes, yes, I know the story."

My attention turns back to the play and Bloody Mary has started the song "Bali Ha'I". After she sings the verse:

> *Your own special hopes,*
> *Your own special dreams*
> *Bloom on de hillside*
> *And shine in de stream*
> *If you try,*
> *You'll find me*
> *Where de sky meets de sea,*
> *"Here am I*
> *Your special island!*
> *Come to me, come to me!"*

Cleary suddenly puts her hand over her mouth, leaps to her feet and stifling a sob, runs up the aisle and out of the door of the auditorium. Rose leans over the seat ahead of her and whispers something into Mrs. Fleming's ear and then she and Mr. Griekos quietly get to their feet to follow Cleary out of the auditorium. Rose puts her hand on my shoulder and tells me to stay there and go to the party with the Flemings. I nod and they leave without another word.

I stay for the rest of the play, trying to enjoy the play and music. However my mind keeps going back to Cleary. What is wrong?

Finally, the music ends and the curtain closes before the cast returns to the stage to collect their standing ovation.

After the clapping has died down and people begin to leave, I move to the row ahead of me and sit next to Mrs. Fleming, who gives me a kind look, but I can tell she really wants to ask me about Cleary. It wouldn't do any good, as I don't know anything. After a short time of small talk, Missy and Debbie come down the aisle to tell us that they are ready to go to the party at Oak Lawn.

My heart is in my throat as I walk along the brick walkway toward the huge house. As with the Christmas party, we are met at the door by a butler who relieves us of our coats. I leave my boots on one of the several doormats lined against the wall and pad into the living room in my stocking feet.

The room is packed with people. Most of the people are cast or band members and their families, others include those who worked behind the scenes or sold tickets. I spy what I am looking for, the buffet, and work my way over to it. Platters of fruit are scattered about on the table, along with finger sandwiches. After fixing myself a plate, I make my way over to the dessert table on the other side of the room. I find pieces of coconut cake, coconut pie, cookies topped with coconut, and coconut pudding. I decide to come back later to get my dessert. Trying to find a place less crowded, I end up in the music room on a fold-out chair. As with the Christmas party, every inch of the house is decorated. Everywhere palms have been set around the rooms. Tropical plants, some fake, some real, are hanging from the ceiling. Fake tropical birds are perched here and there, and sounds of the ocean can be heard throughout the house.

While I am enjoying my food, I look up and see Chris Webster enter the room. He is no longer in the uniform from the play, just jeans and a sweatshirt. His blonde hair hangs down and is still slightly damp from a recent shower. He looks like most any other seventeen-year-old boy in the room. What was it that seemed to upset Cleary about him? Chris looks about the room and seeing me staring at him, asks "Did you like the play?"

I reply that I did and tell him that he did a good job. He smiles in reply and, not seeing who he is looking for, turns and leaves the room. I decide whatever Cleary was upset about couldn't involve Chris.

I have been keeping an eye out for Old Mrs. Vanneste, and so far I haven't seen her. There are so many people milling about, I find myself relaxing. I think to myself that she must have known Debbie is part of the cast and yet she had been invited to the party. Of course Debbie wasn't living with Cleary, a woman she publicly loathed. I suddenly remember what I had told my friends in school about Mrs. Vanneste. I quickly shove the thought from my mind. I sincerely doubt a woman like Mrs. Vanneste would ever hear of the goings on of a class of ten and eleven-year-olds.

I finish off my plate and take it to the table where the dirty dishes have been stacked. While my mind is busy thinking of which coconut dessert I want, I do not pay attention to the woman ahead of me at the dessert table. I see her pick up a small plate holding a piece of coconut cake and turn around and…Horrors! It's Mrs. Lydia Vanneste herself!

She looks at me with light blue eyes that seem to stare right through me. "Ahhh, its young Mr. Thorpe. I wondered if your sister would be bringing you. I think you need to know that I am planning a long talk with your father when he gets back in town."

I gasp and forgetting entirely about dessert, I take off running across the room and don't stop running until I am at the front door. I yank open the door and realize I am only wearing stockings. I look around the foyer and see the closet door. I open it and go in and shut the door and sit on the floor and burst into tears. I don't know how long I sit there before the door opens and shuts and the light is switched on.

It's Debbie and she sits down next to me. "What in the world is wrong?"

I stop sobbing long enough to blow my nose on the paper napkin I have discovered shoved in my pocket when I had gone through the buffet line. "Oh Deb! Mrs. Vanneste is going to talk to Dad!"

Deb gives me a puzzled look. "What *are* you talking about? Why would she talk to Dad?"

"I said something about her…"

"It was *you?* You're the one who started the rumor about Mrs. Vanneste being a mass murderer?"

Now it was my turn to look at her. "Oh I just said she killed a relative." I blew my nose again and after thinking for a few seconds, "I guess I did mention she killed a few others…"

"Kev! My own brother! What in the world made you say something like that?"

"I was upset at the other kids making fun of Cleary. How did you hear about what I had said?"

"Kev, the story is all over town." She shakes her head at me and gives me a disapproving look. "I can't believe Dad would tell you such a stupid story."

"But he did!" I insist.

She ignores my protests and hauls me out of the closet. She tells me to put my boots and coat on and to go outside. "We'll come get you when we're ready to leave." With that she stalks off and rejoins her friends. I receive a pitying look from the butler who retrieves my coat from the closet as I struggle to put my boots back on. I walk out the door and take the walkway to the wall that surrounds the perimeter of the estate and sit down on the cold sidewalk and wait.

I have a long wait. It is over an hour later when the Flemings and Debbie find me huddled on the sidewalk. I can tell from the look on the faces of the Flemings that Debbie has told them what crime I have committed against the town matriarch. I sit in silence as Mr.

Fleming drives out to Raven Hill to drop me off. The house is dark except for a lone light over the sink in the kitchen.

"Should I come in?" questions Mrs. Fleming, who is squinting out the windshield for some sign of life in the huge house.

"No," I say quickly as I throw open the door of the car. Whatever is wrong with Cleary, I don't want Mrs. Fleming nosing around. Plus Cleary and the Griekos don't know what I have said about Mrs. Vanneste; at least I don't think so.

They don't pull away from the house until I open the kitchen door and wave good-bye before shutting the door again.

I find a note on the counter, near the sink. I quickly scan it. "Kev. We didn't think you would be hungry, but help yourself to anything in the fridge. We are in our apartment if you need anything. Please do not disturb Cleary. She does not feel well and went to bed early. See you in the morning. Rose"

They are right, I certainly don't have an appetite. I push the kitchen door open and make my way quietly up the stairs and go into my bedroom and shut the door. I glance in the mirror and am horrified to see my face is still red and puffy. I am relieved I have entered the house without running into anyone.

It is only eight o'clock, but I change into my pajamas and wash up in the bathroom across the hall. I climb into bed and switch off the lamp. I lay there for nearly an hour, not a bit tired, but can't face another minute of this day. I start when I hear someone walking quietly down the hallway and down the stairs. I figure it is Cleary making her way to the kitchen for a snack until I hear the kitchen door open and close. I stand up and look out the window to see a dark figure crossing the snow-covered lawn and disappear into the woods.

I'm not sure what grips me but I realize I am alone in the house and it will probably be my last chance to find out what is in that box in the attic. It is crazy, I know, but I am in so much trouble already that getting into more trouble doesn't seem possible. Pulling open the top drawer of my nightstand, I feel around for the key. Finding it,

I run to the attic door and open it and shut it behind me. I stand there in the dark and almost pull on the string to turn on the light when I realize that it might be seen from outside. Then I remember that the woods blocks the sight of the house and all I can hope for is that the Griekos don't decide to look up at the house from their apartment. Of course they might just think it is Cleary looking for something in her attic.

I pull on the string and the light floods the stairway. I run up the stairs and in the gloom I can just barely make out the box on the shelf over the window. I stand on my tiptoes and gently lift the box off the shelf. I carry the box carefully to the bottom of the steps and take the key out of my pajama top pocket and insert it into the lock. I gently turn it and am immediately rewarded with a snap as the lock springs open. I hold my breath as I slowly open the lid. I am somewhat disappointed, as all I can see are a few photographs, military medals, and momentos that seems to consist of menus of restaurants. I pick up the small stack of photographs and hold up the first one to the light of the single bulb. The first photograph I examine startles me. It is a young man in a uniform. The young man bore a remarkable resemblance to Chris Webster. I quickly realize it isn't Chris but what was it about his eyes staring out at me? I have seen these eyes before. Then the picture of Lydia Vanneste as a child flashes in my mind. The photograph flutters from my fingers and lands back into the box. It is then that I notice a heavy sheet of paper that is folded in three parts. I lift it out and slowly read the words. Silently I fold it back up and place it back in the box and replace the photographs on top of it.

After replacing them I have to reach up and wipe the tears off my face. I am surprised that I have tears left after the events earlier that day, but after what I have just found, they easily flow again. I shut the lid and turn the key, locking it. I quickly replace it on the shelf and run down the steps, shutting the light off on the way. I open the attic door and listen. Nothing. I scurry down the hall and find Cleary's bedroom door open. She isn't back yet, and knowing this might be my last opportunity to replace it, I hurry over to the dresser. I find my way by the light of the moon that shines through the windows and open the bottom drawer on the jewelry case and set the key inside and run out the door and down the hall as fast as my feet will carry me. I shut my door and dive into my bed and pull the sheets over my head. I bury my head into my pillow and cry myself to sleep.

CHAPTER 18

❀

I wake up the next morning when my alarm clock rings in my ear, jolting me awake. I roll over and turn it off and sit up in bed. I feel exhausted. I rub the sleep out of my eyes and get slowly out of bed. I wash and dress for the school day before making my way down stairs. Only Mr. Griekos is in the kitchen, making me a breakfast of bacon and eggs.

"Feeling OK, Kev?"

"I'm just tired," I lie.

"I really enjoyed the play yesterday. Tell Deb she did a really good job when you see her next."

"Sure."

After several minutes of silence he continues, "So, how was the party at Oak Lawn? Lydia sure knows how to throw a party."

Thinking about that woman staring at me and telling me she has to talk to my father only makes me want to change the subject.

"Where is Cleary?"

His back is to me but I can see his shoulders slump. "She isn't feeling well. I don't think you should disturb her."

I want to tell him that I know. I know why she is so upset. I know everything. But I can't tell him how I had found out. I can't say a thing. I can't even tell him that I am in big trouble for spreading the rumor about Mrs. Vanneste either.

I push the scrambled eggs around on the plate as Mr. Griekos keeps up a lively conversation with himself. He finally stops and asks, "Are you sure that you are all right? Perhaps you should stay home from school today."

"Oh no. I'll be fine. I'm just tired."

"Well, OK. If you need to come home, just give me or Rose a call and we'll come get you."

I nod and glance at the kitchen clock. "It's time to go." Actually I have plenty of time, but I just want to get away from his questions.

He drops me off in front of the school and reminds me to give him a call if needed and I assure him that I will. I hesitate before entering, I find that I don't want to face my classmates either. What if they know about Mrs. Vanneste knowing I had spread the story about her blowing up people? What if they know about me crying in the closet last night at the party? And of course, I have plenty of guilt feelings that go along with my opening that box last night too. I sit at my desk, bracing myself for the worst. But it never comes. Instead my salvation was to come in the form of a baby, Fair Emily's baby.

The news that our own Emily had given birth the day before in Chicago has just now reached Traverse City. It is the only thing anyone is talking about. It is a boy, but no one has heard what his name is to be. I have no idea when I might see the baby, but I already love him sight unseen.

That afternoon I am picked up by Rose who keeps up a lively chatter all the way home and until it is time to eat supper. Rose hands me three plates and asks me to set the table while she finishes draining the spaghetti.

"Three plates?"

"Yes. Cleary isn't feeling well. She won't be down."

I don't say a word. The guilt of what I have done, what I know, weighed even heavier on my shoulders.

The Griekos and I sit down to eat together. They keep up a conversation and I answer when I need to.

"Is Cleary OK?" I finally ask.

The Griekos look surprised at the question and look at each other. Rose smiles softly at me and pats me on the hand. "She'll be just fine Kev. Don't worry. She…well, you know she was a nurse in Vietnam. The play just brought up memories."

"Is that it?"

Rose looks quickly down at her plate and nods. But I know that while that may be part of the answer, it isn't all of it.

Rose decides to change the topic with, "I hear Emily had her baby yesterday. I'm sure he is a cutie. I wonder what she will name him?"

"Will Cleary be able to give Emily the baby clothes? I mean she has made several outfits for the baby."

"Of course she will give them to her."

"But she can't go to Oak Lawn," I point out.

Rose shrugs her shoulders. "Emily will come here. She always does."

"You mean when she brought Cleary some food from Mrs. Vanneste's Christmas party?

"How did you know about that?"

"I was sitting on the back stairs when Emily and her husband were sneaking out of the house. Obviously they didn't want Mrs. Vanneste to know where they were going with some food."

"True, they came here and spent some time with Cleary and Sal and I."

I open my mouth to ask exactly *why* Emily would come with food to see Cleary on Christmas Eve, but then I had an epiphany. The Griekos and Emily also knew what was in the box but I'm not sure if Cleary knew they knew. I shake my head; things are getting complicated.

For the next two days the same pattern is repeated. I wake up and am greeted by one of the Griekos who take me to school and pick me up in the afternoon. Then a quiet supper followed by homework, playing cards with Mr. Griekos and then bed. However, on Thursday night, things change.

I have gone to bed early, just after 9 o'clock and I quickly fall asleep. However I wake up shortly after 2 o'clock in the morning by what sounds like gun shots. After a few anxious moments I realize it is the ice breaking up on the bay. I lay there in the dark silence listening to the sounds of the ice. Not only are there sounds like gun shots, but also a low groaning sound that sends chills down my back.

I have been awake for a while when I hear the sound of footsteps coming down the hall and past my door and down the stairs. I listen for the sound of the kitchen door opening but I don't hear it. For some reason this concerns me. I slide out of bed and pull on my robe that I had thrown over the chair at my desk. I open my bedroom door and I can hear a soft sobbing sound somewhere downstairs. I quietly pad down the stairs and peek into the kitchen. No one is there so I continue on to the den and look in. I can see a figure standing in front of the large windows overlooking the lake. Her hands cover her face and her shoulders shake as she sobs. I am afraid to go to her; I don't know what to say. But I find I can't turn around and leave her either.

She jumps as another sharp cracking sound rips through the air. She looks so miserable and frightened that I burst into tears at the sight of her. Hearing me, she turns and opens her arms and I rush into them.

"Don't worry Kevin, it's just the ice breaking up. It reminds me of…"

"I am so sorry Cleary! So sorry!"

She hugs me close "What do you have to be sorry about?"

I look up at her tear-streaked face. "I know Cleary, I know."

She stiffens but doesn't speak.

I swallow hard and stifle my sobs and everything bubbles out of my mouth in a rush. "It's because of Robert isn't it? It's because of

Robert that Mrs. Vanneste hates you! It's because of Robert you had to leave the play because it reminded you…"

She gasps and suddenly holds me at arm length. "Kevin! What do you *know?*"

"I looked, Cleary. I took the key out of your jewelry case and opened the box. I know I shouldn't have but I did. I am so sorry Cleary. I know you were married to Robert and that's why you're so sad."

She doesn't say anything for a long time, she just holds me as my tears flood down her robe. Finally, she says "You're wrong Kevin, it isn't because I was married to Robert or even losing him that has made me so unhappy. It's because no one knows I was married to him. I mean the Griekos know, but they are the only ones."

"No one? Not even Emily?"

She gives me a curious look "No. Why would you think that?"

"You talk to her father. You had her wedding reception here."

"I only had the reception here because of the sheep destroying Oak Lawn. As for Frank, I always hope I am his friend, even though I couldn't marry him."

"Could…" I start but Cleary hushes me and with an arm around my shoulders walks me back to the stairs and up to my room where she tucks me back into bed without another word. After she leaves my bedside I can hear her descend the stairs and in a few minutes hear the kitchen door open and close.

I am surprised when I fall back to sleep and don't wake up until my alarm goes off. I quickly wash, dress and go downstairs. Only Rose is in the kitchen to greet me.

"You're face is flushed. I hope you're not coming down with the flu."

"No, no, I'm fine. I just washed my face."

I had hoped to talk to Cleary, but she doesn't appear before Rose puts on her coat and picks up the keys to the station wagon and leads the way out the kitchen door.

All morning I stare out the classroom window, thinking of the night before. Knowing the secret but not being able to say anything has been torture, but now I am afraid that blurting out that I know might have hurt a person I have come to care about.

It is nearly time for lunch when a knock comes at the classroom door. A note is passed from an office worker to the teacher. She opens the note and walks over to my seat. "It says that you are to report to the principal's office and to bring all of your belongings with you."

The chitchat that is going on around me comes to a sudden end as everyone gawks at me openly.

"Call me," Ted whispers as I pass by his desk on my way to retrieve my coat from the coat rack.

I nod numbly.

I enter the principal's office and to my surprise and delight I find my dad sitting in the waiting room. I drop my belongings on a chair and rush into his arms. After he releases me from his hug, he looks at me and says, "I'm sorry Kev, Mr. Snyder called me and told me that he needed to talk to us about something you did."

My eyes open wide. I have a horrible feeling I know exactly what is coming.

We are escorted into Mr. Snyder's office and my dad and I sit in the two uncomfortable chairs across the wide desk from my principal. Mr. Snyder leans across the wide expanse and rests his elbows on the desk. "Mr. Thorpe, I am sorry to tell you that Kevin has been the originator of a horrible lie circulating this community."

My father stares back in disbelief. "What exactly is my son accused of saying?"

"That Mrs. Lydia Vanneste was involved in some explosion that resulted in several deaths. Obviously it's a monstrous lie that has caused considerable pain to this community's most respected member."

My father's head snaps around to look at me. "Kevin! Why in the world would you tell people such a thing?"

"They…"

"Who is 'they'?"

"The other kids."

"Go on."

"The other kids were making fun of Cleary. It just sort of slipped out about Mrs. Vanneste."

"What about Mrs. Vanneste?"

"You know. What you said about an explosion and her relative dying."

A look of shock crosses my father's face as Mr. Snyder leans even further across his desk.

"I am so sorry, Mr. Snyder. I did tell Kevin about an explosion that took place several years ago. I apparently didn't explain all of the details to him as I should have."

Mr. Snyder clears his throat and fidgets with his pencil. "I am sorry to say that I have decided to suspend Kevin from school tomorrow and for the entire next week."

"I would be happy to talk to Mrs. Vanneste and explain the situation to her."

"I have already talked to Mrs. Vanneste. In fact, she was against me suspending Kevin at all. But I feel Kevin needs to be held accountable for his actions."

I find myself surprised that Mrs. Vanneste isn't the one behind my punishment.

Feeling that the meeting is over, my father stands up, "Thank you Mr. Snyder, I will be having a long conversation with my son and he will apologize personally to Mrs. Vanneste."

The men shake hands and my father and I walk out the door together and find his car.

I speak first. "I'm sorry Dad. I know I shouldn't have said what I said. But you *did* tell me that she was involved in an explosion."

He sighs heavily. "Let's not talk about it right now. I have finished my work in Grand Rapids so I am home to stay. Since you won't be going to school tomorrow, I think I'll take Debbie out for the day and we can all go to Detroit and see your Grandparents and everyone. Your mother says everyone is doing great and I'm sure they would love to see the both of you. We can stop in Bath on the way there and I'll explain the explosion. How does that sound?"

I can't imagine why we need to go to some town named Bath for him to explain anything to me, but I keep silent; I am in enough trouble.

"I called Rose and she was kind enough to offer to pack up your belongings and drop your bags off later. Did you have a good time with Cleary?"

I nod my head.

"I guess the other kids were teasing you? I didn't really think about that happening. I guess people see her as rather odd. But I've known her all my life and she has been nothing but nice."

"I had a nice time with Cleary and the Griekos. I really did. I just didn't like it when they made fun of her."

He pats my leg as we pull into our driveway. "Well, you're home now. You'll serve your time, apologize to Mrs. Vanneste, and soon all this will be behind you. You'll see."

I too want to believe all this will soon be behind me. I want to tell my dad the secret of Cleary and Robert, but I sense that confessing to snooping would only get me into more trouble. I also sense that this is one secret that I have no right in telling anyone. I look at my dad and reply, "Sure, I'm sure everything will be fine."

That night after supper my father calls Mrs. Vanneste and tells her that I am looking forward to apologizing to her in person. After a long conversation my father finally hangs up the phone and turns to me. "Well, Mrs. Vanneste is busy planning the Christening of her new grandson. So you can apologize when we go to the reception after the Christening. It's the weekend after next."

"Sure." I gulp.

"Go get ready for bed. We have a busy day ahead of us tomorrow."

I obey. I am rather curious what our plans are, but my father has been tightlipped about our trip and I can only guess what I will discover the next day.

CHAPTER 19

❀

I roll over waiting for the bathroom door to open; signifying that Debbie is done with her morning ritual. The Flemings had dropped her off the night before. I can hear drawers opening and slamming and her wailing, "I can't find anything!" I know what she means. Mr. Griekos had dropped my bags off last night. I hadn't felt like figuring out where everything went, so I simply opened them and left them on the floor around my bed.

It is difficult to believe my time at Raven Hill is over. It seems like I have been there forever, yet it had flown by so quickly. I wonder how Cleary is doing. Last night I had inquired about Cleary, but Mr. Griekos simply answered that she is fine. I hope she is.

After all of us dress and eat breakfast, we get into the car and head out of town. I catch Debbie looking at me and shaking her head.

"What's up with you?"

"You. I can't believe you got suspended from school. Of course I can't believe you told such a lie. You're lucky you weren't thrown out of school for the rest of the year."

"I guess I ruined things between you and Chris, huh?"

"Why you little…" she stammers as she starts pounding me with her fists.

"Who's Chris?" my father asks from the safety of the driver's seat.

"Webster. Chris Webster. He was in the play with Debbie."

"Oh. OK Deb, stop hitting Kevin. And Kev, you're in enough trouble."

My sister smiles smugly and sits back in her seat and seems to enjoy the rest of the trip.

We are nearly to Lansing when my father gets off the expressway and heads east. We travel a two-lane highway until we come to a small town where a 'Welcome' sign announces the town of Bath.

My dad drives around, traversing several streets that are lined with mostly small, modest homes. He seems to find what he is looking for because he pulls into a parking spot and we all climb out. Looking around I can't imagine what a small town like this has to do with the likes of the grand Mrs. Vanneste. Before us lies a large, grassy lot with an odd structure standing in the center.

"What is that?"

"It's a coppala. It used to top the school that stood on this spot."

From the tone in his voice I can tell that there is a story behind his simple answer. But I don't ask for him to explain and I wander up to the structure and circle it. The coppala must stand about ten feet high and if the three of us had linked hands, perhaps we could have encircled its girth. I notice a plaque with a picture attached. It shows a brick school with what looks like this very coppala perched on its top.

"What happened to the school?" Debbie finally asks.

"Well, in 1927, on the last day of school before they started summer break, a man blew up the school."

Debbie gasps, "What!? You're kidding? Right?"

"I wish I was. He first murdered his wife and burned his house and farm down. Then he went to the school where he had previously set dynamite in the school's basement and set it off with a timer. After the explosion he called the superintendent of schools over to him and he set off the explosives in his car, killing the both of them."

Both of us kids are speechless as my father continues, "The blast killed thirty-seven children, seven adults and injured dozens. It would have been even worse, but the dynamite that was to go off a short time later didn't explode."

"Why would a person do such a thing?" Debbie murmurs as she surveys the green grass before her.

"I don't know if there really is a simple answer for something like this. The story is that he was losing his farm and blamed the community."

"Why would he blame the community?"

"Well, the town built a new school. A school that had grades 1st through 12th under one roof. They called them 'consolidated' schools and in order to pay for it they raised taxes on the residents of Bath. He blamed the high taxes for his financial problems."

After walking around the empty lot that is now a park, we decide to walk the short distance to the downtown area that consists of a few buildings on either side of the road. We look into the few windows of the buildings that are occupied before we head back to our car. Dad then drives the short distance to the Bath cemetery. We walk among the headstones and my father points out the stones that have May 18, 1927 as the death date or the stones of children and teenagers that just list the year of 1927. We walk in silence until we come to the headstone that is in the shape of a life-sized Labrador Retriever and Debbie pats the animal on its head.

"How neat! I wonder if he liked to hunt or just liked dogs?" My dad and I smile; it seems to be the only light hearted moment we have had that day.

I run my hand over the cold, hard haunches of the dog and finally decide to ask my father the question that has been in my head since we came to this tiny town. "But what does Bath and the school explosion have to do with Mrs. Vanneste?"

"After her break-up with Horatio Calloway, Mrs. Vanneste came to live with her cousin who was fresh out of college and had started her first teaching position here in Bath. She died in the explosion. I understand Lydia was one of the first persons on the scene and was slightly injured when the man blew up his car. I think the explosion was the final straw after her break up with Cleary's father that sent her to the sanitarium."

Poor Mrs. Vanneste! I feel awful for Mrs. Vanneste. Back in 1927 she wouldn't have been the grumpy old lady I know. No, she would have been much more like the young girl that stared defiantly out at me from that picture or the pre-teen who had skipped rope on that railroad car. And here I spread the story that she had been responsible for something as horrific as this!

My father put his arm around my shoulder. "I'm sorry, Kev. I should have told you the whole story and then you wouldn't have gotten confused and thought Lydia could have done something like this. But it's hard. Impossible to explain…" he waves his hand toward one of the headstones "something like this to a child your age. I wish I could keep something like this from you longer."

I suddenly think of Cleary and her reaction to the ice breaking up on the bay, "It's like war. It's so horrible you don't want to talk about it."

My father gives me a curious look. "Yes Kev. It's a lot like that. What made you think of that?"

"Cleary was a nurse in Vietnam. Did you know that?"

"Of course. I guess she talked to you about that?"

I shook my head. "Not really. I just know her brother and Robert Vanneste died there."

He nodded sadly, "Yes they did. They were both my friends."

We walk again around the area for a few more minutes before we get back into the car to continue on our way to Detroit. On one hand I am relieved to find out what had really happened and Mrs. Vanneste had nothing to do with it, but on the other hand I felt crushing guilt for spreading such a horrible lie. I sit back in my seat and watch the world whiz by the window. In a way I am looking forward to apologizing and having this terrific weight taken off my small shoulders.

An hour later we pull up in front of the home of my grandparents. My Grandma, hearing the car, comes out to the front porch to greet us.

"I'm happy to say you're just in time for dinner. Your mother is at your aunt and uncle's house and should be here any minute." She throws an arm over my shoulders and the other arm over Debbie's shoulders and hugs us close. My dad retrieves the luggage from the trunk of the car and follows us inside the house.

We find Grandpa sitting in the easy chair with a walker situated nearby. He grins and waves us over to him. "I'm sorry, it's still hard to get to my feet."

We happily lean over the chair and give him a hug and peck on the cheek.

"Are you feeling better?" Debbie worriedly asks, looking at his rather pale face.

"Ah yes. I broke both legs you know. Got the casts off two weeks ago and just starting to get used to my legs again." Debbie and I take a seat on the couch opposite him when he asks innocently, "So how are things with you two?"

"Well, I was in the musical "South Pacific" and Kevin here got tossed out of school for a week for slandering the good name of the town matriarch."

I open my mouth to repute what she has just said, but I realize I don't know what the word "slandering" means.

"I heard all about it from your mom. Well, Kevin, we all make mistakes and I'm sure it will never happen again."

I nod and give him a wide grin. Debbie rolls her eyes. Just then we hear a car pulling into the driveway and we run excitedly to the door and welcome our mom as she walks through the door. While she gives us each a hug, she gives me a weary look that tells me that she isn't as forgiving as Grandpa.

The next day, Saturday, we spend visiting with Aunt Mary and Uncle Henry and our cousins. The youngest two children weren't hurt, but everyone else had broken some bones and other injuries. My oldest cousin, Jason, proudly lifts his shirt to show off his surgical scars. "See? I had to have my spleen out." I wrinkle my nose at the large scar on his abdomen. "And look here." He points to a long jagged line under his eye. "I almost lost my eye!" I am not sure if I should be horrified or impressed as he shows off his scars. I guess in the end I am pretty impressed.

Late that afternoon, after we have returned to Grandma and Grandpa's house, I sit on the double bed in the spare bedroom that my mother has been sleeping on for the last three months. She is packing up her belongings and I watch her in silence.

She sighs heavily as she snaps one of the suitcases closed and sets it aside. She finally looks at me with disappointment in her eyes. I speak first "I'm so sorry Mom! I really didn't mean for Mrs. Vanneste to find out what I had said about her."

"Kevin! The point is you don't say those things to begin with!"

"That's what I meant," I insist.

She sighs again and sits next to me on the bed. "Kev, in the last few months I've learned what's important and what isn't in this world. I guess all you really did was hurt Mrs. Vanneste's feelings. Feelings are important, but other things are more so, like the well being of your loved ones. Do you understand?"

I nod and suddenly think of Cleary and Robert. "I'll apologize to Mrs. Vanneste when we go to the Christening next weekend."

"Good. So what all did you do at Miss Calloways? Did you have good time?"

I assure her that I had enjoyed my visit and told her all the fun I had had playing cards with Mr. Griekos and being served a hot breakfast every morning.

My mom shakes her head. "Don't get used to that, young man!" She sobers for a moment. "I have to admit that I wasn't too thrilled when your father suggested for you to stay with Cleary. I know she was a good friend of your Dad, but she has always been seen a little odd by the people around there. I don't know, she just seemed a little sad to me." My mother opens the drawers of the dresser and adds, "It's a shame she never married and had children."

I open my mouth to reply that she had been married, but catch myself in time. I am suddenly so afraid of spilling the beans that I jump off the bed and run out of the room. My mother turns back towards me just in time to see me disappearing around the corner. "Then again, maybe she is the lucky one," I heard her mutter.

CHAPTER 20

After we return home, the rest of the week goes by quickly. True, I am suspended from school, but my mother calls my teachers and I have to complete my schoolwork every morning under the direction of my mother. The afternoons are spent helping her complete the spring cleaning around the yard. I am jubilant when the weekend arrives and I am given time off for good behavior.

On Sunday I put on my best shirt with my suit because it is the Christening of Emily's baby. The Christening will take place after church services are over and will be followed by a party at Oak Lawn. My father has strongly suggested that I approach Mrs. Vanneste after the Christening and before the party and offer my apology.

The church is overflowing with spring flowers this morning. I think they are left over from a wedding the day before, but my mother assures me they are all for Emily and the baby. I can see Emily sitting in the front pew next to her husband and parents. Old Mrs. Vanneste was also with them. But I don't see any baby.

Across the aisle, towards the back, I can see Miss Calloway sitting with the Griekos. Before the service begins I catch her eye and wave to her and she smiles back. She is dressed prettily in a flowered dress and on her face is a happy, yet determined expression.

After the last hymn is sung, the people who have not been invited to the Christening slowly file out and those who have been invited stay in our seats. I sit there quietly reading the weekly bulletin when I happen to look up and see Old Mrs. Vanneste turn in her seat and stare towards something near the back of the church. I turn to see what she is looking at and find that the object of her attention is...gulp! Miss Calloway. Miss Calloway is sitting alone, the Griekos having left, and staring right back at Mrs. Vanneste. I glance back at Mrs. Vanneste who is struggling to get to her feet, but is prevented from doing so by her son who has a tight grip on the hem of the suit jacket she is wearing. I am afraid of what might happen, but just then Emily, who had left the church early, comes through the back doors carrying a squalling baby dressed in mounds of frothy white material. Susan, Emily's mother, walks behind her with a diaper bag. Seeing her granddaughter, Mrs. Vanneste resumes her seat.

After a few minutes of Emily and her husband Jack consulting with the minister, the ceremony begins. The organist plays a few selected pieces of music followed by the minister saying a few words before calling Emily and her husband forward along with another couple that my mother informs me are Jack's brother and his wife and they will be the godparents. The minister then sprinkles water on the forehead of the baby, which causes him to cry even louder and mumbles a few more words that I can't hear. When that is finished the minister carries the baby and stands in front of the congregation and holds the baby up while announcing, "I am happy to welcome little Benjamin Robert Van Raalte to our church family." He went on to say a few more words but I have stopped listening. I lean over towards my father."That was her uncle's name." My father seems surprised that I would know that and whispers back, "Yes, his name was Robert Benjamin. It's nice she is honoring her uncle this way." I look back towards Cleary, who is wiping away a few tears from her face.

After the last hymn is sung we all file out into the sunny, cool air of early spring. I notice Cleary has already left the church, probably to avoid Old Mrs. Vanneste. We then drive the short distance to Oak

Lawn and find a parking space a block away and follow others on their way to the mansion.

Debbie puts her arm around my shoulder and says loudly, "This is our third party in the last four months at Oak Lawn. I could get used to this!" She then leans in closely and says in my ear, "You had better make this a good apology. Because if we don't get invited to another party I swear I'll kill you."

I give her a dark look and shrug her arm off my shoulders and walk faster down the brick path to the front door. The butler is there to greet us and take the few wraps that people are wearing on this surprisingly warm day. We proceed into the living room where most people have gathered. We see Old Mrs. Vanneste talking to a young couple and my father grasps my hand in his and says softly, "Come on, we might as well get this over with and enjoy the rest of the party."

I can only nod as he pulls me over towards her. We have to wait for a few minutes before she ends her conversation and the couple walks away. Old Mrs. Vanneste is wearing an obviously expensive lavender two piece suit and her silver hair is piled into a smart twist on the back of her head. She taps her cane on the floor in front of me. "Well, what do you have to say for yourself young man?"

I move my lips for a second but no sound comes out. I clear my throat and finally come out with, "Mrs. Vanneste, I am sorry I said those things about you. I didn't mean to hurt your feelings." Her sharp blue eyes soften for a moment before she responds, "I guess you heard the lie about me from that Miss Calloway. Well, I understand. I'm sure she said a lot of mean things about me. People shouldn't say those kind of things in front of children."

I am old enough to realize that the old woman has shifted the blame for what happened to Cleary and away from me. Somehow I find the nerve to look up into her face and reply, "Actually I don't remember Cleary ever saying anything mean about you. My Dad told me the story of the explosion."

With that she snaps her head up and trains her steely blue eyes on him. It was the first and only time I would see my father's face turn red. Now it is his turn to stammer and find the right words. "Ahhhh…Actually I did tell him of the explosion in Bath and somehow I didn't explain it well and he got confused…" he finishes lamely.

She sighs heavily and looks at me again "Well, I accept your apology young Mr. Thorpe. I am happy to see some young people with manners." She manages a smile towards me and then gives my father a shake of her head and adds; "I would have expected more from you, Thomas." She then turns and greets another group of guests. It is obvious that the matter is settled and we have been dismissed.

"I'm sorry Dad, I guess she is mad at you now."

"Oh don't worry, she was angry with me on several occasions when I was a kid."

"She was?"

"Oh yes. We kids would trample the flowers, take off for hours without telling anyone where we were going, slide down the banister. Oh yes, she yelled at us a lot. But Lydia really was good to our gang of kids. We would camp out on the lawn, use the Vanneste boats, and fix meals for us. I know you don't believe me, but she was always kind hearted to us. It's just since Frank didn't marry Cleary and Robert died that she has become rather gruff. Who knows? Perhaps if Cleary had married Frank she wouldn't have become like this."

I want to say that I know why Cleary couldn't marry Frank but I don't dare. Inside I struggle to keep the words only in my head and not on my tongue. How can I know that the secret will remain just that, a secret, for only a few more minutes?

"Well, let's go see the baby before we get something to eat. How does that sound?"

I nod in agreement and we make our way to the east drawing room where, we are informed, Emily is holding court and showing off the newest Vanneste, never mind that his last name is Van Raalte.

We find Emily sitting on an overstuffed loveseat with the baby displayed on her lap. It takes several minutes for my dad and I to get to the front of the line. I lean over the baby who is for once silent but flailing his arms and legs around in the oversized white, frilly gown. Emily grins excitedly at me. "So Kev, what do you think of Benjamin?"

"Why do you have a dress on a boy?" I ask quite frankly.

Emily laughs. "It's a Christening gown. Even boys wear them. It's been in the Vanneste family for over a hundred years."

Just then I feel someone move behind me and place her arms around my shoulders. It is Cleary. "It's nice to see you again Kev. Emily, did you know Kevin was staying with me for a few months?"

Emily nods. "I did hear that. Did you enjoy Raven Hill? Quite a nice place huh?"

I assure her that I did have a pleasant stay and then Emily pats the seat next to her."Cleary, please have a seat and I'll let you hold Benjamin. I'll have Jack find the photographer and have him take a few pictures of the two of you."

Cleary looks rather surprised but pleased as she sits down next to Emily and takes the baby into her arms and looks down at the little face peering up at her. "I can tell you're going to have blue eyes and blonde hair and look just like Robert," she says softly.

"What are *you* doing here! Give that baby back to Emily and leave Oak Lawn this instant! You are *not* welcome in this house!"

I look behind me and find Old Mrs. Vanneste bustling into the room with her son and daughter-in-law running behind her trying to calm her down.

Emily jumps to her feet and stares into her grandmothers eyes and says in a slow, low voice, "I don't ever want to hear you talk to my Aunt like that *ever* again."

The old woman steps back like she has been slapped. "Whhhaaaat did you say?"

"I said I don't want you to talk like that to my Aunt ever again. Do you understand me Grandmother?"

Cleary is still sitting on the loveseat with Benjamin in her arms with her mouth agape.

Now it is Mrs. Vanneste who is trying to find words to say. She searches Emily's face but it is obvious that only the truth will suffice.

"How did you find out? Did *she* tell you?"

"I found those cuff links and the tie clip one day when I was playing with your costume jewelry and read what was inscribed on them. I asked my father if it was true and he said it was."

Mrs. Vanneste then turns to her son who has finally caught up to her and stands by her side. His wife nervously stands on his other side clutching his arm. He nods in agreement with his daughter and then adds "Robert told me in a letter that they had married and he couldn't wait for his tour to be over and they could have a proper wedding reception and tell everyone their wonderful news."

"And you told Emily?"

"I wasn't going to lie to her."

"I should have thrown the damn cuff links and tie clip out. Why didn't I?" she asks out loud more to herself than to anyone in the room. Then she stomps her cane on the floor and stands up straight and turns her attention to Cleary who is still sitting there with a shocked look on her face. "I still have a few things to stay to you, Clarissa. This is just one more example of how everyone in this town points at me and says, 'Isn't she mean to that poor Miss Calloway? Poor old woman never got over being dumped by Miss Calloway's father and then she never got over Miss Calloway dumping her oldest son!' Well, I'll tell you what I never got over Clarissa, I never got over burying *my* son and *your* husband!"

I think the woman's face will explode, but she is just warming up. "That's right, those cuff links and tie clip were sent here before Robert died. I'm the mother, I'm thinking they will write or call me with the news. Do you? No! My son is killed and I hold a wake for him.

Sure you show up and pay your condolences to the family, saying you're home because your brother died too. I wonder if he hadn't died about the same time, if you would have shown up at all!"

Her shoulders heave with emotion but I can tell she still has one more thing to say. "Didn't it ever seem odd that instead of burying Robert next to me, where there was only room for one more, I had him buried nearby where there was room for another? I waited and waited for you to come to me and tell me that he was your husband, but you never did. You just let me bury my son and let everyone think I was a nasty old woman because I hated you. I couldn't help it! Every time I looked at you, I just kept thinking Robert deserved better than someone who wouldn't even claim him after he died!"

Tears roll down Cleary's face and fall onto Benjamin who somehow has fallen asleep with all of the commotion going on around him. She then stands up and hands the baby to Emily and looks at Mrs. Vanneste and says simply, "You're right, he did deserve better." With that she slowly walks out of the room.

For several minutes everyone in the room remains silent, shocked with what has just happened. Mrs. Vanneste wipes her eyes and says in a tired tone of voice. "I think I will lie down for a while. Please see to the guests for me." With her cane tapping along, she makes her way out of the room and heads for the back staircase.

It isn't long before the news circulates around the party and I know from personal experience that this bit of news will be all over town by the next day. As we drive home I look blankly out the window. I feel bad for Cleary, but I also feel bad for Mrs. Vanneste. I suddenly realize why she had acted as she did toward Cleary. I can't say as I really blame her.

❖   ❖   ❖

I swing my legs absent-mindedly and my mother lightly taps my leg to remind me to stop that for about the tenth time this morning. The air in the church is oppressive and the scent of the flowers that fill the sanctuary is choking me. I lean forward and peer through the heads ahead of me to catch sight of the persons seated in the front row. I doubt if I'm the only one who is curious to catch a glimpse of the sight of Old Mrs. Vanneste and Cleary sitting side by side in the front pew. My mother pokes me and I listen as the minister drones "…And most of all we are here to celebrate the memory of Robert Benjamin Vanneste who died in the service of his country. He was the younger son of Donald and Lydia Vanneste and the husband of Clarissa Calloway…"

I lean away from my mother and whisper in my father's ear, "Did you know they were married?"

"No. I didn't know but I'm not really surprised. I always knew there was a strong connection between them. I just thought it was because she had saved him from drowning."

I settle back in my seat and listen to the rest of the service. In the weeks since the Christening the two women had obviously worked through the situation and had come together to arrange this memorial service for Robert. Perhaps the revelation of the secret wouldn't be an end but a beginning.

CHAPTER 21

The old car grinds to a halt before the garage at Raven Hill. I step out of the car and remove my light jacket and open the back door and toss it on the back seat. I carefully remove the black robe that hangs from the garment hook. I quickly put it on and zip it up and then reach for the mortarboard that is on the back seat and place it on my head. It wants to slide off so I hold it in place while I use the other hand to place the tassel with the "Class of '88'" insignia to hang on the right side of my face. With one hand I make sure the gold cords hang evenly on each side of my chest. Once I am certain that I look presentable I walk towards the kitchen door. I don't even have a chance to knock before the door is flung open and Rose is standing there to welcome me into the kitchen.

"I thought I heard someone. I told Cleary you were here and she should be down in a minute. Sal had to run to the store for some last minute items and should be here shortly. Stand still! I want to see you in your robe!" She holds me at arms length and looks me up and down, "I swear Kev, you get taller every time I see you. I see you're graduating with honors."

I nod and smile with pride "High honors". I had worked so hard the last four years that I was thrilled to have earned a high grade point average.

"So what are you going to study at U of M?"

"Business. I plan on getting my CPA."

She laughs. "You picked that as your project in school, remember?"

How could I forget? "Yea, and I only got a **B** on the project!"

Just then the kitchen door opens and Cleary bounces into the room. "I'm so glad you could come today Kevin!" I notice she is holding a small, wrapped package in her hand and she holds it up for me to see. "I have a graduation gift for you."

"Oh you didn't have to do that Cleary."

"Sure I did."

Rose interrupts our conversation. "Why don't you two talk outside until dinner is ready? It's too nice to stay inside."

Cleary grabs my arm and pulls me toward the door. "Let's talk outside until dinner is ready."

We walk out to the lawn so that we can enjoy the warmth of the spring sunshine.

"Cleary, before I go away to school and since I probably will never come back," I begin in a teasing tone, "will you please tell me why such a beautiful house and grounds has a name like 'Raven Hill'?"

Cleary laughs. "It's a rather dreary name isn't it? Well it's not really that mysterious. My grandfather picked out this area and there was a nest of crows on the grounds. The construction began and the birds weren't too happy and showed their displeasure by attacking the builders and stealing small objects. My grandfather thought they were quite audacious and decided to name the place after them. Except, of course, he thought "raven" sounded more glamorous or British or something. My grandmother tried to suggest other names, but somehow the name stuck. So any more questions for me since you're going away and never coming back?"

"Actually, yes. Several."

She studies my serious face for a minute before holding out the small present that she has been carrying.

I take the small package from her and slowly unwrap it and find a small jewelry box. I open it and inside is a pair of cuff links and a tie clip. They are silver and inlaid with mother of pearl. I can tell they are well made and expensive. I raise my eyes and look at Cleary.

"Turn over the tie clip," is all she says.

I lift it out and read the inscription on the back. "For my husband, Robert. Clarissa."

I stare at the words for a minute before looking back at Cleary. "Are these the cuff links that Lydia…"

"…Was talking about at the Christening? Yes. Those would be them. After Robert and I married…oh let me start from the beginning. That would be easier wouldn't it?"

I nod and together we begin to walk about the great expanse of lawn.

"As you know Robert and I grew up together. He was about five years younger than I was and that's a lot of years when you're a teenager. I honestly never thought that much about him until that boating accident when I pulled him out of the wreckage. After that I would visit with him while he was recuperating. We would read the same books, talk about the same movies. I found out that when I had to go back to college that fall that it was Robert that I would miss, not Frank. I know that sounds horrible. It was just so expected that we would marry. The whole town thought we would. Granted Lydia didn't like me much at first, me being the daughter of the man who had dumped her so unceremoniously so many years before. But gradually she came to see what a match it would make. My parents liked Frank, but didn't push the matter. So Frank and I dated for two more years before he graduated from college and proposed. We decided to get married the following summer after I graduated from nursing school. I spent that summer before the scheduled nuptials here at Raven Hill and saw a lot of my friends and especially Robert. Of course he just saw me as a friend and his future sister-in-law, but I realized he meant a lot more to me. I went back to college and realized that if I had feelings for anyone other than my fiancé, including someone of Roberts's age, then I shouldn't be getting married to Frank or anyone else. So that Christmas I had a heart to heart chat with Frank and told him everything. Well, not everything, I didn't tell exactly *who* had initiated these thoughts and feelings. So we did the mature thing and called off the wedding. Unfortunately the adults didn't handle the situation as well. Lydia was beside herself. She took it as a personal slap in the face and took it out on me and my parents and my brother. My brother Ezra and Robert were best friends and Lydia forbid them to hang out together."

At the mention of her brother's name, Cleary stops and takes a deep breath before she continues on with her story. "I graduated that spring and took a job in Indiana, anything to stay away from Traverse City. The following year Ezra and Robert graduated from high school. I had gone home to attend the graduation ceremony and found that my feelings for Robert hadn't gone away. Frank had already married Susan, so I guess he got over me quickly enough!" Cleary adds without any trace of bitterness.

"Robert and I, as friends, did spend some time together on my trip home. Of course we had to hide from Lydia and any people she might know, which is everyone in Traverse City. We used to meet in the cemetery. It was the only private place we could meet in the area. We used to sit on the bench near the Vanneste graves and talk about the future. I guess I'm guilty of helping him and Ezra run away after graduation."

She stops when she sees me raise my eyebrows in astonishment. "You heard right. After Lydia forbade the boys from socializing for their last year of high school, they decided to run off and join the Air Force. They had always been fascinated with flying and after Robert's near drowning they weren't going to join the Navy. Of course when Lydia found out she blamed the Calloways and especially me. I guess she was partly right for once."

Cleary's face turns serious and she looks off over the bay before she continues, "So that is how they ended up in Vietnam together. It was early in the war and people really hadn't started protesting like they would in the later years. It was before they shipped out that Robert stopped by for one last visit. By that time I had moved back to Traverse City after my father had died and my mother was not doing well. We went to the cemetery for our last talk and it was then that he told me that he thought he loved me and when he came back he would like to start dating me. I was thrilled because I already knew I loved him and I told him so. The future right at that moment seemed bright but it didn't last long. My mother passed away and I was left alone in a town where Lydia Vanneste had turned most of the people against me."

"That must have been…horrible," was the only comment I could think to say at that moment.

"Oh, the worst and the best were still to come. Ezra wrote to me and suggested that I come to Vietnam as a nurse. That way I could at least see Robert and him when they were able to obtain a leave. So I did. I just up and quit my job and joined the military with the understanding that I would be stationed over there. I guess distance does make the heart grow fonder because during his first leave Robert proposed and a month later we each took a week off and flew to Japan and married in a simple ceremony. It was in Japan that I ordered the cuff links and tie clip as a wedding gift. They had to be engraved so I left them there with my Traverse City address and Robert's name."

"So no one knew you were married except Ezra?"

"I thought so at the time. I have since found out that he had told Frank. You see, he expected to come home and have another wedding with all the trimmings right here in Traverse City. Frank says that Robert wanted him to do some of the footwork, you know, look for a caterer and photographer, that kind of thing. I didn't know that though. In the meantime the jeweler in Japan had sent the cuff links and tie clip to Raven Hill. Unfortunately he sent it with Robert's name on it and of course the mailman knew where Robert used to live so he sent it to Oak Lawn. Lydia opened it and that is how she knew we had married. She told me later that she had also tracked down the marriage license."

I am afraid to ask anymore. Afraid it will bring up the pain that was hidden for so many years. But I don't need to because Cleary clears her throat and continues, "So we were married for about six months. They were the happiest of my life. Someday if you marry you'll understand. But…but one day the news arrived that his plane had been shot down. He was gone. I didn't know what to do. Only Ezra knew I was married as far as I knew. It took some time to recover…Robert from the scene. I was able to go through his personal affects before they were shipped home. I thought I had removed all traces of the wedding. I forgot about the cuff links until much later but I just figured they had gotten lost in the mail. It was a couple of months after Robert died that Ezra was injured and brought to the hospital where I worked. He was doing well one day and then infection set in and he was gone too. They shipped Robert and Ezra home on the same day. Isn't that odd?"

I do not know what to say so I say nothing.

"I was able to secure a discharge and came home at that time to bury my brother. I wanted to tell everyone that I was Robert's wife, but I went to his wake and took one look at Lydia and I couldn't get the words out. I left Robert laying in his casket in the East room, all by himself. How could I do that?"

At this tears roll down her face and I am suddenly sorry that she is telling me her story. "Please stop Cleary. You don't have to tell me anymore about you and Robert."

She wipes her eyes with her sleeve. "You don't understand, it makes me happy that *I can* talk about Robert. For so long I kept it hidden. You have no idea how happy I am that the secret came out."

"You are?"

"Oh yes, at the time I was horrified and ashamed. But later Lydia and I sat down and talked it out. It wasn't easy. There were things she didn't want to hear and there were certainly things I didn't want to hear. But they needed to be said. She was right you know. I did abandon my husband when he died. I had blamed her for everything and frankly enjoyed the fact that people in town thought badly of her for how she treated me. But I was wrong. Poor Lydia, she hadn't had the happiest of lives and then when I never told her about the marriage and she found out by accident…well, she had every reason to dislike me too. But once the truth was out I found that she really has a heart of gold. It's just been dinged too often in her life."

"I have seen you two mentioned often in the papers together."

"Oh yes, Lydia has dragged me out of the house and out on the town. We have had a lot of fun. I wish we could have more time together, but Lydia has been slowing down this last year."

I reach into the small jewelry box and lift up a cuff link and hold it up to the sun and let the sun bring out all of the colors of the mother-of-pearl. "It's beautiful Cleary. Thank you so much. I just can't figure out why you're giving them to me."

"Well, Kev, I think your coming to stay with me showed me what I was missing. I was lucky, my parent's left me well provided for and I didn't have to work. But I was missing out on life. I really only had the Griekos and a dead husband buried next door for company."

"The Griekos knew about Robert, didn't they?"

"Oh yes. I had finally told them after the funerals were over. I swore them to secrecy. I didn't know Frank and Lydia knew, I just thought it was kind of Frank to keep in touch and even let me watch over Emily for a few weeks."

"I'm going to miss you Cleary. I don't think I will be home much because my aunt and uncle are going to put me to work during breaks and the summers. I'll even miss the blue lilacs," I added as I walked over to a bush and buried my face into it's thick blossoms.

Cleary walks over to stand beside me. "Kev, you know they are really purple. There is no such thing as blue lilacs."

"But…"

"It's just perception. The sky, the water, even the grass all come together and make them special." She cocked her head to the side. "It's like the Calloways and the Vanneste families coming here and Robert and I finding each other. Everything came together to produce something special. But like the lilacs, it was only special in one place and time and it will never come again. Do you know what I mean?"

I nod and she takes my arm and we walk back towards the house. "I bought those cuff links and tie clip for Robert, but since he never had a chance to wear them I'd be proud and happy if you would wear them."

"I'll keep them always Cleary. And I'll always think of you and Robert when I wear them."

"Good. Good." With that we head back to the house.

CHAPTER 22

We sit there in silence for several minutes before anyone moves. I am afraid that I have bored everyone to sleep. But no, Sarah looks up at me from her seat on the ground at my feet. "Oh Daddy, I feel so sorry for Cleary and Robert. But I'm glad she made friends with Old Mrs. Vanneste."

"I am too, hon. She found peace and joy when the secret came out. I'll always wonder what would have happened if she had told it earlier rather than Emily blurting it out when she was upset."

"I'm glad Emily had such ah...spunk."

I laugh at the word she has chosen to describe Fair Emily. "I guess she takes after her grandmother in more than just looks."

Lisa stretches and yawns and I take that as my cue to say "OK, everyone, we've had a busy day and we are going home tomorrow, so off to bed and we had better *stay in bed*," I add with emphasis to my children. Together we make our way through the trees and across the lawn to the house and back to bed.

The sun is barely up before I open my eyes and take a deep breath. I smell sausage and bacon being cooked downstairs. For a moment I am transported back in time and I am ten again and waiting for Rose or Cleary to rouse me from my bed. I quietly climb out of bed and make my way down the stairs like I had so many years before. I push open the door to the kitchen and Mr. Griekos greets me.

"Sal! You're making breakfast for us! You didn't need to do that. We should be making it for you."

He dismisses my words with a wave of his hand. "I'm so happy to have you and your family back to visit Kev. I just wish it was a happier occasion."

"Me too, Sal."

"I guess you heard that I'll be allowed to stay on after this place becomes a hospice."

"Yes, that's great Sal. I know you'll miss Cleary, but you'll have company around."

"Yea, it was lonely after Rose passed on, and now that Cleary is gone, well, it will be nice to see some more folks around. I understand they are coming out today and doing a planning meeting."

"Then I had better get my family up and out." Just as I am about to leave the kitchen the door opens and my children and Lisa, followed by Debbie and my father walk through the door.

"Eating without us?" my father teases.

"Hey I know for a fact Sal makes the best sausage and pancakes, why would I want to share?" I tease back.

After we sit down to breakfast and then clean up afterwards, we reluctantly make our way upstairs to pack. Over an hour later I am packing the suitcases and bags in the two cars that Lisa and I have driven to Traverse City. I am enjoying being alone. Everyone else has returned for one last visit to the beach. After slamming the trunk down, I walk back into the house and walk around the second floor and then around the first floor. I tell myself that I am looking for items my family may have left behind, but I am really saying goodbye. The last room I visit is the living room and I make my way over to a picture hanging on the wall. It's an old picture, showing a preteen girl skipping rope on a railway car. Her flying blonde hair hides her face but I know it belongs to Lydia Vanneste. Lydia had given the picture to Cleary years ago and Cleary had promised it to me when the time came. I reach up and remove it from the wall and look at it for a few quiet moments. I take it out to my car and carefully pack the picture in my luggage to prevent any breakage or damage to the frame. Not wanting to ruin my family's fun quite yet, I walk around to the garden on the other side of the house. I find that the covering has been removed from the fountain and I look at the figure of the little girl holding an umbrella with one hand and her arm protectively around the shoulders of her little brother.

"I hope you're with your little brother and Robert now Cleary. I know you have missed both of them for so long." I take a short tour of the garden and then I hear a truck pull into the driveway. I return to the other side of the house and find Emily with a pair of men I don't recognize. The men pull a large sign out of the back of the truck and place it off to the side of the driveway and proceed to pound on it until it stands on its own in the soft earth.

"What is that?"

Emily, hearing me, turns around and excitedly gestures for me to come closer. I do and look at the sign which reads "Announcing the formation of the Blue Lilacs Hospice Foundation."

"What do you think? We thought we would advertise and get people excited about the community project. The house itself is going to be "The House Of The Blue Lilacs" and will have a plaque honoring Cleary and the Calloway family."

"You're changing the name of Raven Hill?"

"Yes, even Cleary agreed it sounded rather…well…depressing for a hospice. We had talked about it and she even wrote the name change in the charter when she arranged for all of this. In fact, she even told me that you were the one who mentioned the name."

"I did?" I am lost in thought, but then suddenly I recall that day I came to Raven Hill after my graduation from high school. "I guess I did now that I think about it."

"The name fits perfectly. I'll be thrilled to come visit when I can. I hope you can come visit once it opens in a few months."

I nod. I would like to come home and visit Raven Hill or should I say The House Of The Blue Lilacs?

Epilogue

Andrew P. Kehoe was born February 1, 1872 on a farm about four miles outside the town of Tecumseh, Michigan. It is believed he studied electrical engineering in St. Louis, Missouri and Lansing, Michigan and worked on electrical lines before returning to Michigan around 1905. He eventually married Miss Nellie Price and they would remain childless. In 1919 they moved to the Price homestead outside of Bath after the death of her father and Andrew farmed the land.

Around the time the Kehoes moved to Bath, the community decided to build a consolidated school (that is, a school that would teach grades kindergarten through high school). The school opened its doors in the fall of 1922. Andrew Kehoe experienced financial difficulties and blamed the taxes brought about by the new school. In an attempt to keep the costs of the school to a minimum, he ran for a position on the school board and was elected. In another attempt to keep costs down he volunteered to help with the upkeep and repairs around the school in exchange for a minimum charge, or for free.

By late 1926 it was obvious that Kehoe was on the verge of losing his farm due to the back taxes he owed and that his wife was in ill health and often hospitalized. Kehoe saw the new school as the root of all his problems. He also had a particular dislike of the school Superintendent, a Mr. Emory Huyck.

Sometime during the winter of 1927 he began setting dynamite in the basement and crawl space under the school. Since he was a familiar sight around the school, no one was suspicious if they saw him coming or going at odd hours of the day or night.

Sometime between May 16th and the 18th, Andrew Kehoe murdered his wife, Nellie and placed her body in one of the farm outbuildings. He also wired his house and outbuilding with explosives.

On May 18th, 1927 at about 9:45 am an explosion ripped through the Bath school, demolishing one wing of the brick structure. At about the same time explosions and fires destroyed the Kehoe farmstead. Minutes after the school explosion, Kehoe drove up in front of the school and motioned for the Superintendent, Mr. Huyck to come to him. When he reached Kehoe's truck, Kehoe ignited explosives, killing both of them and two bystanders.

Along with pulling out the bodies of victims and rushing the injured to hospitals, rescuers at the school also discovered 504 pounds of dynamite that had failed to explode. The total of the devastation would be 37 children dead, 7 adults dead, and 58 injured.

If you go to Bath today you will find the site of the school has been preserved as a park. The site includes a pavilion, State of Michigan Historical marker and a plaque listing the names of the dead. In the center of the park sits the cupola that once topped the school. A short drive from the park is the Bath Cemetery where several of the victims are buried. Kehoe was buried in an unmarked pauper's grave in St. Johns, Michigan.

Bibliography

Ellsworth, M.J. The Bath School Disaster. 7th ed. Bath: Bath School Museum Committee, 2001

"Life After Terrorism," Detroit Free Press, 9 December 2001, Section J, p. 1J.

Parker, Grant. <u>Mayday: The History of a Village Holocaust.</u> 4th ed. Perry: Parker Press. 1980.

About the Author

Kelly Kathryn Griffin was born and raised in Flint, Michigan. In her writing she enjoys combining her love of history and travel.

0-595-25433-0